Attainment
Book 3.5 in The Temptation Series

K. M. Golland

Cover Design by: Wade Angelo,
Pauze - Design and Multimedia

Copyright © 2013
ISBN: 978-1499580631
Published by K. M. Golland

All rights reserved. This book may not be reproduced, scanned, or distributed in any printed or electronic format without permission from the author. Please do not participate in or encourage piracy of copyrighted materials in violation of the author's rights. All characters and storylines are the property of the author and your support and respect is appreciated. The characters and events portrayed in this book are fictitious. Any similarity to real persons, living or dead, is coincidental and not intended by the author. Except the original material written by the author, all songs, song titles and lyrics contained in this book are the property of the respective songwriters and copyright holders

For the fans who politely, and not so politely, asked for Bryce's voice. This is for you.

BOOKS BY KM. Golland

Temptation (The Temptation Series #1)
Satisfaction (The Temptation Series #2)
Fulfillment (The Temptation Series #3)
Attainment (The Temptation Series #3.5)

Coming Soon
Attraction (The Temptation Series #4)
Discovering Stella

CONTENTS

Prologue	Pg 9
Chapter One	Pg 11
Chapter Two	Pg 22
Chapter Three	Pg 33
Chapter Four	Pg 44
Chapter Five	Pg 55
Chapter Six	Pg 72
Chapter Seven	Pg 80
Chapter Eight	Pg 90
Chapter Nine	Pg 102
Chapter Ten	Pg 119
Chapter Eleven	Pg 129
Chapter Twelve	Pg 143
Chapter Thirteen	Pg 157
Chapter Fourteen	Pg 162
Chapter Fifteen	Pg 179
Chapter Sixteen	Pg 200
Chapter Seventeen	Pg 210
Chapter Eighteen	Pg 222

CONTENTS

Epilogue	Pg 233
Attraction Prologue	Pg 241
Acknowledgements	Pg 243
Author Bio	Pg 245

ATTAINMENT

PROLOGUE

How do you know when you are truly happy and that your life is ultimately fulfilled in all aspects imaginable? Is that even possible ... ultimate attainment? Some people measure their happiness on their level of success, while others measure it on their fortune or ability to live an unencumbered or inhibited lifestyle. Some people even fool themselves into believing that they are truly happy when, in fact, they are just filling a void with a bullshit pretence.

Not too long ago, I was one of those people; deceiving myself into believing my life was what it ought to be. But as I sit here now, looking out the window of my City Metropol building toward my penthouse apartment at City Tower, I feel nothing but ultimate attainment. Today, I can finally say that I have achieved everything I have ever wanted in life. Today, my family becomes complete. Today, I marry the love of my life; Alexis. It is today, after setting eyes upon her three years ago, that I will finally be able to call her my wife.

From that very moment when I first saw her, she stirred something within me that had lay dormant — happiness. But it wasn't until our lips first touched that I knew I would stop at nothing to have her completely. There was just something in that kiss which told me she was the one, something in that instant shifted in me — I needed her; I wanted her.

Wholeheartedly knowing at that point that we were both put on this earth to be together, I realised how I would make that happen. I would show her what she was missing in life. I would show her how it felt to truly be desired and loved. I would show her what her life was supposed to be like — I would show her me ... us ... forever.

PART ONE

My life has just begun

CHAPTER ONE

Glancing ever so slightly toward Alexis who is sitting in the passenger seat of my car, I notice her perform an awkward shuffle of her arse. It is obvious she is uncomfortable — again.

Over the past six months, I have watched what she endures on a daily basis from being pregnant. And during those times, I couldn't help but find myself wondering just what it would feel like. You know ... to be pregnant; to carry a small human being inside your abdomen. Would it feel like you've just eaten one huge breakfast? Or would it feel like you constantly want to squeeze the baby out from between your legs, the same feeling you get when you can no longer hold onto that shit you've been putting off having all day? I guess it could ... it does make sense. Or perhaps it just simply feels like you've swallowed a watermelon ... whole. A watermelon with moving limbs ... and hair?

I shudder at the thought.

Speaking of hair on a baby's head, apparently our little angel has a decent amount of it. According to Alexis, that is the reason why she is burping so much, or, as she puts it: 'Indigestion', Can hair on your unborn baby's head really make you burp? To me, that's like saying the socks I chose to wear today make me fart. It's just ridiculous and completely far-fetched. I don't understand why Alexis feels she needs an excuse to burp, and even when she does belch unexpectedly, I still find her sexy as hell. Probably even more so because she blushes then comes up with her little pregnancy-fib. *Yes, I'm not stupid. Hair on a baby's head cannot make you burp.*

Initially, most of the stuff she told me about being pregnant I had put down to being a pregnancy-fib. Some of it resulted in confusion, or had made me laugh in disbelief, or it had just scared the absolute shit out of me. Like when she'd said that a father could experience 'a sympathetic pregnancy' or more technically put — couvade syndrome.

What. The. Fuck?

I remember her telling me while displaying that cocky, fucking adorable smirk on her face. 'Bryce,' she'd said with one eyebrow raised, 'there's a very good chance you could experience morning sickness, weight gain, sore breasts —' she rattled off. At that point, I'd had no choice but to interrupt her, saying 'I don't fucking own breasts, Alexis. How the hell can I get sore ones? You're yanking my chain, honey.' But no, she was adamant it was true. So, of course, I googled it. Well, fuck me, she wasn't lying. A father could actually experience symptoms of pregnancy.

Now, I've said it before and I will say it again. I will do absolutely anything for Alexis ... anything. Because let's face it, I worship the ground this woman walks on. But experience sore breasts, breasts I don't even have, and labour pain? Screw that. I was born with a dick, and not experiencing childbirth firsthand is a perk of owning said dick.

Alexis' voice slowly becomes audible, tearing me away from my nightmarish thoughts of couvade syndrome.

ATTAINMENT

'Bryce, earth to Bryce,' she says in a singsong tone.

'Yeah?' I ask a little stunned, before gathering my bearings.

'Are you with me?'

'Sorry, I was faraway.'

'It would appear so. Where is faraway?'

I take off my seat belt and turn to face her, noticing her concerned expression. 'Never mind, I'm here now, honey. And it appears that we are here now, too,' I say as I glance around the underground car park of Dr Rainer's consulting rooms.

'Yes, we are,' Alexis murmurs, still displaying an expression of concern. 'You sure you're all right?'

'Really, I'm fine. And,' I say, now directing the conversation to my baby while leaning over to press my lips to Alexis' stomach, 'today we are going to find out if you need a blue room or a pink room —'

'Oh no, we are not!' she interrupts, and gently pushes my head back.

I move against her shove, returning to her stomach. 'Yes, we are.'

'Bryce, I want it to be a secret.'

'Fine, I'll keep it a secret from you.'

'You can't,' she pleads.

'Yes, I can.'

'No, I mean you can't do this to me. It's not fair that you will know the sex and I won't.'

I take her hands in mine and smile at her beautifully distraught face. 'Honey, I'm not waiting to find out what we are having. I want to know. I want to be prepared. If you want it to be a surprise, I promise I won't tell you. In fact, I think I will enjoy not telling you.'

Alexis abruptly removes her hands from mine and shoves me back over to my side of the car. 'I hate you,' she grumbles.

I laugh. 'No, you don't.'

'Grrr,' she growls as she quickly tries to exit the car.

Hurrying out of my side, I meet her and hold her door open as she steps out. 'You fucking love me and you know it,' I say, leaning against it with my ankles crossed while pretending to brush something off my shoulder in a show of cockiness. I really shouldn't bait her, it's just ... I can't help myself. Her little fightbacks are always such a turn-on.

She slowly stands up straight, giving me a little Alexis-attitude. 'Yeah, well that can change.' *Like fuck it can change.*

I waste no time and bend down, gently sweeping her off her feet and placing her on the bonnet of the car. 'No. It. Can't. Change,' I reaffirm, before taking her head in my hands and pressing my mouth to hers.

The remnants of her toothpaste coat my tongue as I thrust it into her mouth, taking possession of her tongue like it's mine. Well ... it kind of is mine; she is mine. My possessiveness forces a moan to escape her which brings a smile to my face. I love how she reacts to my touch.

Sliding one hand to the back of her head, I pull her closer, prompting her tongue to delve deeper. *Fuck!* I want to take her here

... now ... on the Lexus. I know how much she loves being fucked in, on and against my cars.

My cock springs to life, encouraging thoughts of making love to her before our appointment. But I know we can't, we shouldn't. Well, not here, anyway. The thought of anyone seeing her in the throes of passion does not sit well with me. Only I get that privilege.

I reluctantly separate our conjoined mouths and rest my forehead against hers. 'Come on, we need to leave before I strip you naked and run my tongue right down your centre. Believe me, the thought is crossing my mind.'

Her mouth drops open, but she then shuts it again and smiles, refusing to budge by displaying a cheeky grin on her face.

'I'm serious. Come on,' I say, taking hold of her hand and shaking my head in amusement. Alexis, when pregnant, is insatiable ... horny as fuck ... as randy as a rabbit. Hell, she almost wears me out ... almost!

***

Before too long, we are in Dr Rainer's office and Alexis is lying flat on the examination table with an ultrasound image of our baby swirling around on the monitor. Her hand is gripping mine with an intense clasp as we wait for the sound of a heartbeat.

She won't admit it, but I know this is hard for her. How could it not be? It wasn't long ago that we were both here staring at a similar image, that image being Bianca. If fate hadn't decided to be cruel and malicious during that time, Bianca would now be approximately four months old.

I take a deep breath, push aside my sad thoughts and smile at my fiancée. I have to be strong for her, because god knows she is forever putting on a brave face. What Alexis has experienced in the past eighteen months is more than most would experience in a lifetime. Her continual strength and resilience blow me away, together with her ability to take on life's ruthless challenges and not only meet them head on, but somehow find a way to conquer them. When all is said and done, Alexis is simply amazing, and I thank my lucky stars every day that she has agreed to become my wife. Not only that, but she is carrying my second child, and her two children — Nate and Charlotte — have accepted me as their stepfather. I couldn't be more proud.

The rhythmic sound of popping filters through my ears, bringing my gaze back up to the screen. It really is such a wonderful tone, a reassuring one.

Hearing our baby's heartbeat, Alexis lets out the breath she has been holding and tilts her head to flash me one of her earth-shattering smiles.

I lean down to give her a quick kiss. 'Everything is fine, my love.'

She nods.

Dr Rainer records a few measurements on the screen then turns to me and Alexis. 'Baby's heartbeat is still strong at 140 beats per minute. And his or her measurements are consistent with gestation —'

'His? Or hers?' I ask, probably a bit too eagerly.

'Do you really want to find out?' she questions with a curious smile, seeming to know that I do and Alexis does not.

'Yes, although Mummy here,' I gesture to my not so happy looking fiancée, 'does not. So you can whisper it in my —'

'All right! All right!' Alexis blurts out, clearly frustrated. 'I want to know, too.' She crosses her arms over her chest in a show of reluctant surrender.

I have to smile, because she looks so damn adorable. I knew she would eventually cave in. She hates secrets with a passion, especially when I'm the holder of the secret in question.

Gently grazing my knuckles down the side of her face, I smile at her triumphantly. 'You know, you really don't have to find out. I promise I won't tell.'

'Screw you, Bryce Edward Clark. I'm finding out the sex of our baby.'

I laugh out loud. 'There you go, Dr Rainer. We both want to find out.'

'Very well. I'm fairly certain I know baby Clark's gender already. However, I want a better angle just to be sure. Alexis, I'm going to move the ultrasound wand further down and apply a firm pressure. This will help get a better view of baby's genitals,' she explains.

Dr Rainer does as she has just informed and pushes into Alexis' lower abdomen, causing her to wince.

'Are you all right?' I say with concern, glaring at Dr Rainer.

Alexis squeezes my hand. 'Yes, I'm fine. I just need to pee ... desperately.'

I let out a sigh of relief and am thankful Dr Rainer didn't see my unwarranted look of displeasure.

'I'm sorry, Alexis, I know this is uncomfortable for you.'

'Yeah, you can say that again.'

'Okay, nearly done. You do know this is not one hundred percent accurate, don't you?' Dr Rainer informs us, her eyebrow raised.

'Yes,' we both answer simultaneously.

'Good, okay. There we go.' She presses a few buttons which freezes the image on the screen. 'Say hello to your son. You're having a little boy.'

Alexis gets up on her elbows while I lean in closer to the screen. *Fuckin' oath, that's a boy. Check him out!*

'There,' I point to the screen. 'He sure is, and he takes after his father.'

'Bryce, that's your son's leg,' Dr Rainer states in a dry, condescending tone.

Bullshit! He doesn't have three legs ... I quickly re-count. *One leg. Two legs ... that's definitely not a third leg. He most certainly takes after me.* I smile proudly with a knowing nod of my head.

'Bryce,' Alexis says, grabbing my attention, choking on her words and trying to push back her tears. 'We are having a boy. That's our son. Look at him.'

I glance back at the screen. *My son! That's my fucking son! That little blurry image is my living, breathing baby boy.* I turn back to lay eyes on Alexis' beautiful face and realise that life doesn't get much better than this.

ATTAINMENT

***

On our way back to City Towers, I start to think about the things I can organise, change and get ready ... like our son's room. The renovations and rebuild of the penthouse are not far off completion, and it's probably only a few more weeks before we can move back in. After our ordeal with Gareth, I'd tried to convince Alexis to consider moving into a house by the bay, or in the suburbs — wherever she wanted. But she'd wanted to remain at City Towers, assuring me that it just 'felt right', that it was 'home'. Our home.

Not wanting to argue with her decision — because let's face it, it was a fucking brave one — I instigated repairs, renovations and a rebuild almost instantly. In the meantime, though, we have been residing in the presidential villa.

Sadly, pretty much everything on the first floor of the apartment was ruined by the explosion and subsequent fire. The upstairs bedrooms had sustained water damage, but no clear structural impairment. Mainly, the devastation was cosmetic, although Charli was absolutely shattered that her 4Life memorabilia was destroyed. Little does she know that I have arranged replacements and plan to surprise her with them when the refurbished apartment is unveiled.

'What are you thinking about?' Alexis says, once again breaking me out of my trip to "faraway".'

'Our son. Our home. Our future,' I honestly answer.

'And ...?'

I quickly glance at her, curious of her questioning tone.

'And … I have a lot to do. The apartment should be finished in a few weeks and I want it to be perfect before we move back in.'

She reaches over and touches my face. I love her soft touch. 'Bryce, it will be. I have no doubt. Please stop worrying about that.'

I release one hand from the steering wheel and take hold of hers, pressing my lips to her wrist. 'I love you.'

'I know you do,' she smiles. 'And I love you, too.'

Feeling bold and knowing she is in a very good mood, I broach an off-limits topic. 'Are you sure you don't want to get married sooner? I know you want to wait, but —'

'Bryce, we've talked about this. You know I can't wait to be your wife. But after everything that has happened, and with BB on the way, I just think we need to slow down a bit and enjoy the ride.'

'BB?'

'Well … yeah …' She coyly hesitates. *Damn, she's cute.* 'BB … as in Baby Bryce.' She gently caresses her stomach, filling me with so much fucking love for this woman that I can barely breathe.

'Baby Bryce?' I repeat, unable to contain my grin.

'Yes.'

I continue to drive, silence now swirling around us. Every couple of seconds I glance at her, knowing she is watching my reaction.

'You know, Mr Clark,' she says, her tone now lowered and sounding sexy as hell, 'when you smile like that it makes me want to climb onto your lap.'

'Honey, you are a threat to road safety. You really need to get in control of that.'

'Then stop grinning that sex-on-a-stick grin. I just want to lick it.'

'I can't stop. You have that effect on me.'

'I know. So it appears we have a predicament.'

'We do.'

She leans over and slides her hand across my thigh, stopping on top of the hard mound in my pants.

'Alexis,' I growl in warning. *Bloody hell, she drives me wild.*

She gives me a firm squeeze while answering in an innocently sweet voice. 'Yes?'

Swallowing heavily, I rein in the serious wood that is forming beneath her hand. 'You'd better start thinking of all the ways you want to be fucked. Because when we get home, we are going to be performing each and every one of them.'

CHAPTER TWO

Experiencing conflict with one's self, when you think about it, is kind of absurd. But despite that absurdity, we subject ourselves to this illogical torment at more than one point in our lives. Why? I would probably put it down to stubbornness, or the ability to be unyielding, even if that means you go to war with yourself.

I'm no stranger to being at war — figuratively speaking — having fought and won many battles in my life. Battles in business, against family, and even against morality. But fighting a battle against one's self is not a battle you intend losing. The thing is, if you are defeated, then you have only yourself to blame.

***

'Bryce, I know this is hard for you. But you have to talk about your feelings of guilt if you ever want to get past them.'

I look up from my seated position. Jessica — my psychologist and family friend — is sitting across from me with her notepad rested on her lap. She has her reading glasses perched on the tip of her nose and a troubled expression on her face. It's quite obvious to me that her concern is due to the fact I am not openly discussing what happened with Gareth as she wishes I would.

We are both sitting in her office, which is situated on Bourke Street in the CBD of Melbourne. It's a quaint office, furnished with soft colours, unobtrusive ornaments and feel-good artwork, purposefully placed to make her patients feel comfortable, relaxed and, unbeknown to them, unguarded. I have been here many times and am aware of my deceptive surroundings; they don't fool me.

'What if I don't want to get past my guilt? What if I don't deserve to?' I respond with determination.

'Guilt is felt not only by the guilty, but more so by those who feel they deserve it when, in fact, they don't. Guilt can be a humble, yet deceitful emotion.'

'Jessica,' I sigh, deflated and tired as a result of this session's conflict. 'I know you are trying to help. I know you are trying to make me see that Gareth's death was not my fault. The truth of the matter is ... it was. I abandoned him when he really needed me and, on top of that, I nearly lost Alexis in the process. I deserve this guilt. Please, just let me bear it.'

She places her notepad on the seat next to her and removes her glasses. 'Gareth's death was not your fault. If it was, then it would equally be mine. Actions have consequences, consequences have results and sometimes those results are devastating, as in Gareth's case.'

Leaning back in my chair, I close my eyes and run my hands through my hair, the pain and memory of my mentally ill cousin's demise still too brutally raw.

'Bryce, look at me,' Jessica says with a soft, but authoritative voice.

I open my eyes and meet her gaze.

'I'm going to ask you to think about something and then I want to discuss it next week.'

'Sure,' I respond flippantly, with a tinge of arrogance. My intention is not to be an arsehole. After all, she means well. It's just that I'm exhausted and want to get home to Alexis and find solace in her warm embrace. Alexis keeps me grounded; she always has and I hope she always will.

'What you're experiencing is known as "unhealthy" or "inappropriate" guilt. I want you to look at the situation from a different point of view, put someone else in your shoes. Take Lucy for instance. What if it were her? Would you find her just as responsible for Gareth's death? After all, she too is his cousin. She knew what you knew. She had just as much influence as you —'

'Jessica,' I snap, 'leave Lucy out of this. It —'

'Bryce!' she interrupts, as abruptly as I had. 'Just think about what I'm saying and we'll talk about it next week.'

I stand up, not happy with her request to 'pretend' to put Lucy in my place. Gareth's death had nothing to do with my sister. 'Fine, I will see you next week. When is Alexis due to come in next?'

'Alexis and I have arranged monthly visits now. She tends to listen to my advice and not be so sceptical of what *you* may feel are unorthodox suggestions.'

My eye involuntarily twitches and I clench, then release, my fist. *Bloody hell, she is on a tirade today.* 'I'm glad to hear my fiancée is dealing with the situation and finding a way to put it behind her. Thank you. The last thing she needs is to feel any stress in her current state.'

Jessica stands and makes her way toward her desk. 'Well, she is not the only one.'

'Goodbye, Jessica,' I respond, contemptuously. 'I will see you next week.'

'Bryce,' she says, not looking up, 'you know that, despite your stubbornness, your mother would be proud of you.'

I sigh. 'You tell me this every time.'

'Well, it's true. She would, and you need to hear it.'

I head for the door without looking back and give her the reply that I always do, 'Thank you.' Except this time, I don't really mean it.

***

A few weeks later, we are standing on the threshold of our newly refurbished apartment with my hands covering Alexis' eyes.

'Are you ready?' I ask, drawing out the unveiling of the renovations.

She urges me forward. 'Yes! Yes! Come on, let's go in.'

Releasing one hand from her eyes, I turn the handle on the door, opening it for us to walk inside. 'Keep them closed until I say, all right?'

She huffs. 'Yes, okay, you are such a control freak.'

'And your problem is?'

'Bryce Edward Clar—'

'Okay, okay,' I chuckle, while holding her back against my front and slowly shuffling us along the entryway of the apartment.

Leaning down, I slowly and softly whisper into her ear. 'You can open them, my love.'

I tilt my head around to get a clear view of her reaction, watching her eyelids flutter and the expression on her face morph from anticipation to amazement. It's not as if she was blind to what the newly refurbished apartment would look like, because she did, after all, help redesign it. But I guess seeing it in actuality for the first time, together with the extra little bits and pieces I organised without her knowledge, is the cause of her happy astonishment.

She steps forward and gazes over the lounge area. 'Oh, Bryce, it's ... it's ... wow! It's wonderful.'

The layout of the apartment is still much the same, except now there is no step down into the lounge. Alexis wanted to minimise the number of steps in consideration of the rolling, then crawling, then walking little person on his way. The other noticeable change is the softer colour palette throughout the lower level, and the now child-friendly furniture — no sharp, sleek lines or edges.

Where there had been shades of grey, white, black and deep blue, there are now cream, beige, fawn and chocolate brown. I'd arranged for new family photographs to be enlarged, framed and displayed on the walls, together with replicas of the cushions Alexis went a little cuckoo over when she left Rick. I'd even arranged for some Twister carpet to be laid in my new recording studio, although it was no longer really fitting to label it a 'recording studio'. You see, it is now a larger room containing many new toys. Not man toys ... but child toys, including the carpet.

Before Alexis has a chance to move further into the apartment, I seize her hand gently and spin her around, stepping her backward until she's stopped against the entryway wall, my prurient intentions now made clear by the pressing of my raging hard-on against her hip.

'I believe we need to break in this freshly rebuilt wall,' I suggest seductively, pinning her arms above her head and grazing my lips across her ear.

Thoughts of the first time I had her pressed to this very spot flit across my mind, and it's obvious to me that I want her now just as much as I wanted her then ... probably even more.

She takes in a sharp breath, pushing her plump tits into my chest before exhaling slowly. 'What did you have in mind?' she purrs.

Fuuuuuck, I love it when she teases me with her sultry voice.

'I think a complete rehash,' I murmur as I lightly lick the crook of her neck, 'of our first time together is a very good start.'

'Start?' she questions, her voice still low and sexy. 'We have to pick up the kids from school soon, Bryce,' she adds, lacking conviction.

Pulling away from her, I look at my watch then lean back in, stopping only centimetres from her mouth. 'There's a lot I can do to you in the space of an hour,' I say as I watch her lips and how she has no control moistening them with her tongue.

'Good,' she smiles, 'I'm looking forward to it.'

Not wanting to waste any time, I slide my tongue into her mouth, relishing her luscious warmth and silky feel. An uncontrollable growl resonates from within me, intensifying our fervour and increasing my need to bury myself inside her. To say

I'm completely attuned to her body's needs is an understatement. I know what she wants ... likes ... needs.

Now feeling her legs weaken, I release one of her hands and hold her hip to steady her and, almost instantly, her newly freed hand finds the back of my head. The tightened grip on my hair fucking exhilarates me.

'Would you like sex up against the wall again?' I ask in a whisper.

'Yes, I'm fucking thirsty.'

I pull away, entertained by her response. Obviously, I was not referring to one of our favourite cocktails, the one which inspired this passionate position in the first place.

She notices my paused state, giggles, and pulls me back in for a kiss. 'I'm kidding,' she mumbles. 'Now, get on your knees. If memory serves me correctly, you were all about tasting, not admiring.'

I shake my head at her sassiness and begin to unbutton her silk blouse, finding her perfect tits with my hands. Kneading them with heightened hunger, I allow my fingers to massage the plump flesh right before pulling down the cup of her bra and taking her nipple into my mouth. The soft peak hardens at my touch, eliciting my desperate urge to flick it with my tongue.

A sharp, uncomfortable yet fucking sensational ache ripples through my head as she suddenly grips my hair and tugs ferociously, indicating her approval of my tongue's pursuit.

'You like that?' I murmur around her wet nipple.

'Uh huh.'

'What else do you like?'

Her hands glide down my shirt as she makes her way to my belt, their journey south such a turn-on. She finds the buckle and, wasting no time in unlatching it, has my cock in her hands within seconds. 'This ... I like this,' she answers.

Fuck! The feel of her warm hands on my shaft stimulates me even further. 'So you fucking should,' I growl, a determined new hunger rolling out of me. I allow her to caress my cock for only a few seconds longer before my impatience wins over and I strip her of her clothes.

Taking a step back and stepping out of my own pants, I hungrily take in her gorgeous pregnant form. Her swollen belly is so fucking beautiful that it has my dick twitching with excitement, knowing that in mere seconds my hands will be caressing what I see in front of me.

I raise my eyes to her chest. The rhythmic rise and fall has me intoxicated, together with her eyes which have now become heavy with desire. It is almost the exact same look she pierced me with the first time we were in this position.

'You still, and always will, fucking take my breath away,' I say as I cup her cheek.

She turns into my hand and closes her eyes, and it's this small sign of pure love that has me dropping to my knees before her.

Alexis' hands find my hair, the corners of her mouth lifting in a provocative grin. *Fuck! That look does me in every time.*

'You want me to taste you, don't you? To run my tongue in between your legs while you tug on my hair?'

'Yes,' she breathes out, 'yes, I do.'

Grabbing my head, she threads her fingers through my hair and coaxes me forward, her yearning desperation now eagerly prompting me to spread her legs and nudge her clit with my nose.

Alexis sucks in a breath and then exhales. 'Oh, Bryce,' she breathes, as her head drops back against the wall. 'Yes, I do want that. I want it now.'

God! I fucking love it when she moans my name. The sound of her quivering approval of my actions always gives me assurance.

Sliding my tongue out, I drag it across her soft skin, sampling her already aroused pussy, the taste — fucking delightful. I could eat her slowly all day. The taste of her at the tip of my tongue is sensational.

Her fingers dig into my scalp in response and, at the same time, my grip tightens on her hips. I swirl my tongue and coax her hips to roll against my mouth. She obliges and lifts her leg, draping it over my shoulder, prompting me to increase my tongue's ferocity as it laps and flicks at her. I could seriously devour her sweet flavour for hours. Listen to her pant for hours. I could, quite simply, stay like this for hours.

'Bryce, I ... I ... oh, god,' she cries out as her body tenses, then shudders while I hold her tight as she comes on my face — one of my favourite things imaginable.

Sucking her clit into my mouth one final time, I follow it with a tender kiss then proceed to stand.

'I need you inside me, now!' she demands, her desperation evident.

Given no time to taste her nipple again, she impatiently grabs my face and directs her mouth to mine, getting a taste of her own arousal on my lips. Being a man who loves to eat pussy, there's just something so incredibly sexy when a woman tastes herself on my face and, when Alexis does it, I could honestly die a happy man.

Separating from her hungry kiss, I spin her around and splay her hands on the wall, then gently coax her into a bent position. My cock throbs with expectant release as I open her up, driving deep inside her. Slowly, I slide back out, tantalising her with my hard length. I know she loves a good tease.

'Does that feel good?' I question between slow thrusts.

'Yes.'

'Do you want it harder?'

'Yes.'

'Are you still thirsty?'

She laughs. 'No.'

I snigger, then proceed to slide in and out of her at a faster pace. In and out, in and out, the warm walls of her pussy massaging my shaft as I glide back and forth.

'You feel so fucking good,' I rasp before reaching forward and cupping her bouncing tits.

Noticing her arms weaken as she holds herself up against the wall, I release one breast and wrap my arm around her waist, supporting her.

'I've got you. Just relax.'

Her body slackens just a little, and her head drops back onto my shoulder. I let go of her breast, brace my hand against the wall, and seize her mouth with my own.

My efforts to refrain from ejaculating become impossible as the sensation is just too great, and I explode into her, filling her as I pulse with pleasure. Our climax melts into one as I continue to roll against her, slowing down and steadying not only our stance, but our breathing as well.

I slide out of her and turn her back around to face me, catching the elated joy radiating from her in the form of a satisfied smile. She wraps her arms around my neck and rests her forehead against mine.

'Why are you so happy?' I question, already pretty sure of the answer.

With a sexy as hell lift of her eyebrow, she takes a hold of my tie and tugs me toward the lounge. 'One room down, at least five to go.'

CHAPTER THREE

One hour was not enough time to complete Alexis' plans for the five rooms. It was, however, enough time for both the recording studio and the master bedroom. Never would I ever say no to her, but damn, was I glad we only had an hour. Any longer and my dick would've fallen off.

In the beginning of the pregnancy, Alexis' sexual appetite was non-existent, and it was completely understandable considering what happened during that time — she was traumatised for a few weeks following Gareth's death. The thing about Alexis, though, is she has an incredible ability to put on a brave face and deal with life's hurdles, as she puts it.

During those initial weeks, we comforted each other, both of us trying to move past the explosion, and I say the term 'move past' with some reservations, 'moving past' not being easily achievable. It wasn't until approximately a month afterward — and in amongst our comforting — that our sexual urges returned, our intimate moments helping heal the unspoken words of the tragic event. Then, for the weeks that followed, Alexis' morning sickness reared its ugly head, halting our recently restored libidos. *Why it is called morning sickness bloody stumps me. It's never just the mornings.*

Shortly after her constant need to vomit disappeared, her sexual desires increased tenfold. Now, don't get me wrong, I'm certainly not complaining. Her physical presence still drives me wild. It's just

... my dick fails to let my brain know that at times it is fucking whacked and in need of a rest.

***

'I can't believe you had Twister carpet put in,' Alexis laughs while watching the passing traffic on the Tullamarine Freeway. She turns to face me with a mischievous grin. 'You know, as soon as I've popped out BB, I'm challenging you to a game ... naked.'

We are on our way to collect Nate and Charlotte from school and then surprise them with the completed apartment.

'Why wait till after you give birth to challenge me?' I ask, curiously. I'm surprised that considering her current sex drive she hasn't penned in a game for this evening.

'Because you will have an unfair advantage.'

'How's that?' I chuckle while noticing her eyes spark wide.

'Because I can't easily twist and manoeuvre with a child growing within my womb.'

Before I can answer her, she shouts at the top of her lungs. 'Hey! Quick! Pull into 7-Eleven.'

Her sudden outburst shocks the shit out of me and has me veering into the service station. In a slight panic, I bring the car to an abrupt halt. 'What! What's wrong? Is everything okay?' I ask, fear gripping my insides as I reach over and place my hands on her stomach to inspect her for signs of distress.

'I need a Slurpee. A big one! Ooh, I hope they have bubblegum flavour,' she says with excitement while patting my slightly trembling hands before unbuckling her seat belt and climbing out of the car. Just before closing the door, she pokes her head back in. 'You want anything?'

Letting out a long sigh of relief, I respond. 'No. I'm all good.'

As I watch her lightly waddle through the shop doors, I drop my head to the steering wheel in exasperation. *Jesus fucking Christ! She will be the death of me.* Talk about giving me a heart attack and all for a frozen, crushed ice drink, saturated in sugar syrup. *Bloody pregnancy cravings.* When Alexis was pregnant with Bianca, she preferred potato chips dipped in ice cream and, as disgusting as that had been, I could stomach the notion and satisfy that particular craving for her when required. However, the shit she has been eating this time around nearly has me dry retching. I mean, who the hell eats pickles on toast with cheese and mayonnaise? And did I mention I caught her dipping a carrot into her glass of chocolate milk last week?

She walks back to the car, happily sucking on her Slurpee.

I smile. She is just so incredibly cute. 'Happy now?' I ask as she sits back in the car and buckles her seat belt.

Alexis sucks her straw, slurping loudly, then smiles back at me. 'Yep.'

'Good.'

She tilts her drink toward me. 'You want some?'

'No. That shit is basically liquid sugar.'

'And your problem is?' she asks while stirring the mixture around, seemingly unperturbed by my factual health statement.

I glance over at her, the sides of my mouth rising in a smug grin. 'My problem is that it's not good for you.'

'BB likes it. Look ...' she points to her stomach, her expression happily cocky, 'he just high fived me.'

Wearing a pair of maternity jeans and a tight fitting grey top, she is all baby-belly.

'Wait for it ...' she says in anticipation.

I humour her and wait, staring at her tummy.

'Ha! See?' she giggles as her tummy jerks ever so slightly, showcasing my son's movement. 'You like Slurpees just like Mummy does, don't you, BB?' she coos in her mummy-baby voice.

Seeing her stomach move like that fills me with a feeling of complete awe, love and astonishment. I could watch it all day. I remember back to the first time I felt BB kick. *BB? Bloody hell! I can't believe she has me referring to my son as the letter B squared.* Annoyed at myself for allowing such a ridiculous nickname for my unborn son, I decide I really need to do something about it sooner rather than later.

Bringing my gaze back to her happy face, I go to complain about the absurd name but am halted as I take in the joy radiating from her while she rubs her tummy.

'Mummy likes the bubblegum and cola flavour, BB, but next time we will try grape. What do you reckon?'

Her hand jerks again and we both laugh. I decide now is not the time to bury the nickname BB and, instead, return to my recollection of when I first felt my son move. It was shortly after we found out that he was a boy. We were lying in bed after just having a bath together, and Alexis was playfully singing 'Kiss You All Over' by Exile, because I had only just moments before kissed her all over. She'd started the chorus then paused mid-word .... 'He kicked!' she'd blurted out, looking at me as though being internally booted was extremely pleasurable. 'Quick! Quick! Give me your hand.' She'd then grabbed my hand and pressed it against her stomach. The wait for movement was the weirdest anticipation I had ever felt. I knew what a baby kicking my hand was like, because I had experienced Alexander do it to Lucy. But waiting to feel the first movement of my own child was ... well, it was surreal. Exciting, but strangely tense.

When that first bump finally nudged my hand, a sensation of sheer fucking joy had spread through me like wildfire. My child was alive, growing and playfully moving around inside the woman I love. I'd felt the joy from the smile plastered across my face travel to the heart pounding in my chest and right down to my feet which had been twitching with excitement. *Best bloody experience, ever!*

Sitting in the car at the 7-Eleven car park and fixing my stare toward Alexis' stomach where my son is happily practising his martial arts skills, I reach over and gently lay my hand across her bump. She looks up at me and her expression changes from cheeky playfulness to one of heartfelt love.

Placing her hand over mine, she asks our son to move again. 'Daddy wants a high five, BB.'

We wait for what seems like minutes when, in actual fact, it was probably only seconds. Our hands jerk in unison, causing my heart to pound with excitement. *Ah, there it is.*

'Good boy,' I praise him then gently fist-bump her tummy.

Alexis interlaces our fingers together then rests our hands on the centre console of the car and, with her free hand, lifts the Slurpee to her mouth, smiles and takes another loud gulp. I shake my head and grin, clenching her hand a little tighter to indicate a sense of amused affection. It's the little things like this without spoken words that I cherish with her. We fit each other so perfectly.

***

After picking up the kids from school, we head home. As we step into the elevator, I hit the penthouse button and stand back. Instantly, Nate questions my choice. The kid doesn't miss a beat; he is so switched on.

'Are we going to check the renovations?' he asks, curiously.

'No, even better,' I reply, waggling my eyebrows.

Nate wrinkles his forehead, then delighted understanding appears on his face in the form of wide eyes. 'It's finished? Are we moving back in?' he asks, looking from me to Alexis then back again.

Charlotte pauses in her dancing to non-existent music and shoots her head up. 'What?'

'I don't know, Bryce. Do you think they are ready to see their new home?' Alexis teasingly asks.

'Hmm, not sure,' I respond, going along with her charade. 'They may not like it.'

'Is my room pink?' Charlotte squeals, jumping up and down. 'Oh, I hope it's pink ... even pinker than last time. I love pink. Wait! I like purple too. Is it purple?'

'You are just going to have to wait and see Charli-Bear,' Alexis states with a smile.

'I don't care what colour my room is, as long as it's not pink ... or purple ... or maybe even yellow,' Nate adds.

'Good, 'cause yours is white and blue, little fella,' I say proudly. 'Carn the mighty Cats!'

I watch his face as his eyes search mine for the slightest telltale sign that I'm bluffing. Nate is a one-eyed Bombers supporter like his mum.

'Mum,' Nate says hesitantly, 'please tell me he's joking.'

I glance at Alexis, trying not to laugh and give myself away. I wonder for a moment if she'll play along and tease Nate, or if she'll cave and stay true to her beloved football team. The inner struggle is evident on her face, and I can't help chuckling at her attempt to prevent it from screwing up.

'Nate, my little man,' she says with gritted teeth, while giving me that sexy fucking determined glare. She stands straight and smiles satisfactorily at me before turning her head to face her son. 'Would I ever let Bryce decorate your room in anything other than the Bombers colours?'

Nate sighs with relief. 'No. You wouldn't.' He then turns to me, and a spark of satisfaction appears to surge through him as he fires a shit-eating grin in my direction. 'When you least expect it, Bryce, you may find a clown sleeping in your bed.'

Alexis bursts out laughing. I, on the other hand, do not find that little threat funny at all.

'Really?' I ask Nate.

He just nods. *Yeah, I wonder who he gets his cockiness from.*

'Bryce,' Charlotte interrupts, her sweet angelic voice laced with concern. I feel her hand gently clasp mine. 'Clowns aren't real, you know. And neither are ghosts, or witches.' Her look of sincerity is both adorable and ... well ... humiliating. Here is a seven year old girl telling a thirty-seven year old man not to be afraid of clowns because they aren't real, when in fact they freakin' are. In this moment my testosterone levels sink dramatically. *I'm a fucking coulrophobic pansy.*

I pull her to my side and give her a hug. 'Thanks, Charli.'

Alexis, who is still trying to refrain from laughing at my awkward I-have-no-balls moment, winks at Charli. Fortunately, the doors to the elevator open. We all step out and Alexis and I hang back, my arm around her shoulder and hers around my waist. We watch excitement filter through the kids as they explore their new surroundings.

'It's just like before, but it's not,' Nate says, displaying an expression of slight confusion.

'I don't know about the brown, Mum,' Charlotte says.

'What's wrong with the brown?'

'Brown is poo colour.'

Alexis laughs. 'It's also chocolate colour.'

Charlotte spins around slowly with her hands on her hips. 'Yeah, but it's not pretty.'

'We don't want the lounge area to be pretty,' I explain.

'Why not?' *Because it's a goddamn lounge, not a fairy palace.*

Alexis squeezes my hip, then lets go. 'If you want pretty, Charli, go see your room.'

Charlotte squeals that high-pitched, burst-my-fucking-eardrums squeal that she is good at, then makes her way upstairs. Nate, Alexis and I follow behind.

The new staircase spirals round in a large curve, deliberately designed that way so it feels like you are walking up a hill rather than a steep incline. Alexis was adamant when we discussed the new designs that she did not want a vertical staircase. And I honestly can't say that I blame her. I think her fall from a year ago still plays on her mind. It probably always will.

Nate calls out from his room, 'Sick!' and I know immediately what he has just found.

'Oh my god!' Charlotte squeals and, again, I know why.

I turn to Alexis, stopping her in her tracks. 'You take Charli. My ears can't handle her vocal range. I'll take Nate,' I say, before hurrying off to Nate's room. His surprise is far more appealing to me than Charli's replacement 4Life memorabilia.

When I walk through his door, he is already opening the boxes. 'These are awesome!' he says, sheer delight covering his face.

I'm fully aware of how awesome they are, having wanted to try one out for days. 'These are the Walkera HM Airwolfs,' I explain to him.

Nate rotates one of the boxes, taking in the picture. 'Sweet!'

He has no idea just *how* sweet these babies are.

Nate and I sit on the floor of his room, wasting no time in putting the remote control helicopters together. Nate hangs on every word that I say as I instruct him in the assembly of the aircraft. Appreciation and fondness fill me when I look at him, as I see his mother's determination and intelligence, not to mention he has her blue eyes. From the moment I met Nate — that time he came to visit his mum's place of work — I found it easy to form a bond with him. He has so much of Alexis flowing through him and possesses an uncanny ability to read most situations. He really is a smart and loving kid.

'Spin that rotor blade there, Nate,' I instruct.

He does what he's told, then smiles as it spins effortlessly. 'It works!'

'I think we are done,' I say in response and get up from my seated position on the floor.

'Thanks, Bryce. I like doing these things with you.'

The honesty in his words and on his face pulls at my heart. I have no doubt that I love him like a father does. But at the same time, I am fully aware that he has a father, a father who loves him dearly. One thing that I never want to do is step on Rick's toes where Nate and Charli are concerned, but that doesn't mean I cannot love them and show them that in my own way.

'You're welcome, mate,' I say as I scruff his hair with my hand. And, as always, he jerks his head away playfully. 'I like doing these things with you, too. Now, let's get these babies up in the air where they belong.'

ATTAINMENT

We place them down on the desk and take a step back, pointing the radio transmitters in their direction. With a hum and a buzz, both of them hover off the desk. I take control instantly, circling it around the room. Nate, however, requires a little longer to perfect his new piloting skills. Surprisingly, though, he takes a lot less time than I expected he would need and before I know it, we have them flying beautifully out of the room. Nate follows me into the passageway, our eyes trained intently on the hovering choppers.

Alexis and Charli duck out of our way with a scream.

'Shit! Sorry,' I smile apologetically.

'My bad!' Nate chimes in, a little less remorseful.

Alexis shakes her head and pulls Charli to her side. 'I knew those things were a bad idea. Did you have to buy two of them?'

'Actually,' I reply with a smirk while keeping my vision solely on my helicopter and slowly walking past Alexis and Charlotte, 'I bought four.' I head for the stairs, Nate in tow.

'Four! Why four? I don't want one,' Alexis exclaims, with a little disgust.

'It's not for you.'

'Who's it fo—' She cuts herself off and sighs. 'Bryce, BB's not even born yet.'

CHAPTER FOUR

The buzzer to the door sounds, indicating Rick's arrival to pick up Nate and Charli for the weekend.

Standing in the kitchen, I finish preparing a spinach, cheese and tomato omelette for Alexis' lunch, the dish full of protein, folic acid and magnesium, which I found out is not only good for her but also good for our baby.

I wipe my hands on the tea towel and toss it on the benchtop before heading into the lounge. When I walk into the room, I spot Rick behind Alexis, his hand on her shoulder and the other pushed firmly into her lower back.

Neither of them seem to notice me at first, and as I stand there watching him place his hands on her, assisting with whatever the fuck he is assisting with, it makes my blood boil.

'Is it there?' Rick asks her.

'Yeah,' she winces. 'It's not as bad as when I carried Charli, but it still hurts.'

'Thought as much. I could tell straight away when I walked in that it was bothering you.'

Not being able to stand there any longer and watch their exchange, and wanting to know what is hurting Alexis and why Rick knows about it and I don't, I make my presence known. 'Is everything all right?' I ask, desperately trying to curb my resentment.

Rick drops his hands and takes a step back just as Alexis straightens and stretches, arching her back and poking out her tummy. The discomfort on her face is obviously present. *Where the fuck has this soreness come from?*

'Yeah,' she murmurs, unaware of the fact that what I just witnessed between her and Rick has unsettled me.

'Bryce,' Rick says with a nod of his head while extending his hand.

The last thing I want to do is shake the fucker's hand, wanting to break it instead for providing relief to my pregnant fiancée's back. I really can't help it. Seeing him with her pisses me off, infusing me with jealousy. But at the same time, I know deep down inside that my response to their interaction with one another is completely unreasonable. Regardless, he still irritates me.

I honestly hate feeling this way. I'm not normally the jealous type. And I'm not afraid to say the reason for this is probably due to the fact I always get what I want. I'm never in a position to be jealous in the first place, so this feeling is somewhat foreign to me, only having felt it one time before — when Alexis was married.

Begrudgingly, I shake Rick's hand as I stand by Alexis and instantly place my hand on her lower back, wanting to remove his touch and replace it with my own.

'Not long to go now,' Rick suggests, nodding toward Alexis' stomach.

'No. Four weeks and two days,' I reply, wanting to reiterate that I know exactly how long.

'Well, yeah, if she delivers on her due date. Alexis tends to go into labour early.' He smiles at her knowingly, and it takes every bit of restraint I have to not knock him the fuck out.

'Dad!' Charli yells, as she comes around the large central pillar that leads to the stairs.

'Princess! Come and give me a big hug.'

Charli drops her shiny pink suitcase and launches herself at Rick.

He lifts her up and places her on his hip, grimacing playfully. 'You've grown again since I saw you last.'

'Well, yeah, Dad!' Charli rolls her eyes. 'I slept four times since then, so I've grown four times. Miss James says you grow in your sleep. Did you know that?'

'I do now. Where's my kiss?' Rick asks, puckering his lips like an idiot.

I notice Alexis smiling at their exchange and it irritates me even more.

'Nate, come on,' Rick yells. 'We've got the footy this afternoon.'

'Coming. Geez, don't go all loco on me,' Nate answers while entering the room.

'Loco?'

'Don't ask, Rick,' Alexis says before giving both Nate and Charli a kiss goodbye. 'Now be good, and I'll see you after school on Monday.'

They hug their mum before fist-bumping me and then walking out the door.

I waste no time in finding out what the hell is wrong with Alexis' back. 'Want to tell me what's wrong with your back?' I ask, my tone deliberately snappy.

She gives me an unsure look. 'I get back spasms. Why? What's wrong? Why are you angry?'

'Because this is the first I'm hearing of it. Yet *he* seems to know all about them.'

I hate speaking to her with such anger in my voice, but I can't help it. Her ex-husband just pisses me right off. Look, there's not a day that goes by where I don't feel a slight bit of guilt for moving in on Alexis when she was married to the scumbag. After all, I'm not a heartless bastard. I think what angers me the most where Rick is concerned, is what he did to her — cheating on her right after she gave birth to Charlotte when she was at her most vulnerable. The thing is, if he hadn't fucked up on an epic scale like he had, she may still be married to him. So it's bittersweet in a way.

'Really, Bryce? You're angry because Rick knows that I get back spasms?' she asks with a roll of her eyes.

Her blatant dismissal of my unease at being kept in the dark angers me even more. 'I'm pissed off because *I* don't know about them.'

'Well, sorrrryyy,' she says, sardonically drawing out the word. 'I didn't realise I needed to tell you absolutely everything. How about I make you a list?' She places her hands on her hips. 'Number one ...' she begins, raising her hands and pointing to a finger. 'My feet have begun to swell and look like little bloated piglets. See?' She kicks off her shoe, sending it hurtling through the air and into the lounge. 'Feel free to oink at them, they may respond.'

The notion that her feet can resemble piglets makes me want to laugh, and I feel my anger toward her slipping away.

'Two ...' She points to another finger, clearly not finished with her defensive tirade. 'My nipples are dry and sore and starting to leak colostrum. Would you like to hear more?' she asks, pausing only for a second. 'Good, 'cause I'll give you more,' she continues, not allowing me the option to refuse. 'I have the constant need to urinate. I feel like I could shit a brick. I have heartburn from hell. And I am so hungry I could eat a horse.'

Colostrum? What the fuck is colostrum? And why is it leaking from her nipples?

I don't answer her for a minute as I try to process the list she has just heatedly rattled off, a list I need to get onto. The fact she could eat a horse stands out to me as the first problem I can solve.

My absent reply — I can only assume — frustrates her further as she huffs and starts to turn away. 'They are just back spasms, Bryce. I didn't think it was that important.'

I soften my voice, feeling like an absolute piece of shit for making her upset. 'Honey, everything to do with you and our baby is important.'

She stops, turns back around and sighs, exhaustion clearly present. 'Honestly, they come and go. They haven't bothered me until recently. I used to get them a lot when I was pregnant with Charli, which is why Rick caught onto it straightaway. I'm not deliberately keeping my ailments from you.'

I take the remaining steps between us and place my hands on her shoulders. 'I want to know everything, EVERYTHING that is happening with that body of yours. I can't help if you don't tell me what is going on.'

Wrapping her hands around my waist, she closes the remaining distance between us as she pulls herself to me, the gorgeous bulge in her belly preventing our complete unity. 'Okay, but you can't help me shit a brick, or stop me from constantly peeing.'

'No, but I can dish you up a horse.'

She laughs. 'I know my cravings are crazy, but steed sandwiches are definitely a no-no.'

'What's colostrum?' I ask, my thoughts back to her nipples.

She pulls away and smiles, then lets out an adorable giggle. 'It's pre-breast milk.'

Pre-breast milk? I can't help but look at her breasts.

Suddenly, I feel a slap and a push to my chest and she is no longer in my arms.

'I'm not going to drown you in it, you know,' Alexis deadpans as she walks away.

'What? I ... I didn't say that.'

I quickly take off, capturing her and holding her back to my front.

'You didn't have to,' she says in a sulky voice. 'You looked at my breasts as though they were ready to shoot at you like a fire hose.'

I laugh out loud. 'I did not. Although ...' Feeling her struggle to free herself from my arms, I hold her tighter, her freedom not even an option. 'I'm kidding. No, seriously, I just thought they couldn't leak anything until after BB is born. And speaking of BB, can we please discuss names? I really cannot bring myself to call him that any more.'

'Why not? It's cute.' She drops her head back onto my shoulder and looks up at me with a smirk. 'I was actually thinking of calling him that officially.'

I squint at her, narrowing my gaze and trying to assess whether she is bluffing or not. 'Don't kid a kidder, my love.'

'I'm not.'

'You better be, because there is no way in hell we are naming our son BB.'

She bites the inside of her bottom lip and smiles. 'Fine, but I at least want his name to begin with B.'

'Why?'

'No reason,' she shrugs.

Leaning forward, I plant a quick kiss on her forehead, causing her eyes to close momentarily. I love how her eyelids fall heavy for the smallest of moments when I kiss her. It shows her vulnerability to my touch. 'Okay, the letter B it is. It's a good letter.' I confidently grin at her.

'Hmm, I know,' she moans, arching her head back further, her lips reaching for mine.

Lowering my head so that I can give her what she wants, what I want — what I always want, to taste her — I savour the feel of her sweet, warm mouth and the soft, silky glide of her tongue against mine. She tastes like the most delectable form of oral consumption known to man, and I am the lucky son of a bitch who exclusively gets to consume her.

Regretfully, I separate my mouth from hers and pull away. 'I have a little work to do. Your lunch is ready and waiting for you in the kitchen.'

She pouts, and it's so fucking lovable. 'Thank you... and fine, you important businessman. I have a date with a very naughty priest anyway.'

What naughty priest? This is the first I've heard of Alexis being religious.

I pull my head back from her in slight disbelief. 'Priest?'

'Yes, Father Stearns.'

'Are you Catholic?'

'No. But after reading this book, I'm thinking of possibly converting.'

'What book?'

She laughs and gives me a little shove. 'Never mind. Go, go and do what you do.'

I take a few steps backward in the direction of my office, still confused by this Stearns bloke.

Still laughing, Alexis blows me a kiss. 'Don't look so concerned.'

'I'm not. I'm not scared of a priest.'

As I turn and open the door to my office, I hear her mumble something barely audible until I hear the word clown.

I pause.

'I love you,' she calls out, giggling.

'Hmm,' is my only response.

***

I spend the next hour looking up baby names beginning with the letter B. Let's just ignore the fact that I am supposed to be finalising the complex's involvement in the upcoming AFL Grand Final celebrations, because the thought of giving my son a name is far more important.

'Bailey,' I say to myself. *Nah, too much like Irish cream.* 'Bane,' I voice, but does it have a wishy-washy tone? *Hmm.*

I decide to check the meaning behind that particular name. 'Son of a farmer.' *No, that won't do, although he is the grandson of a farmer.*

I keep scanning.

'Beaver?' *Are you fucking for real, who would call their son Beaver?* 'Bowel?' *Now that's just cruel.* I shake my head and keep reading down the list. 'Boyd.' *Maybe.* It does say that Boyd means blond-haired, and I'm fairly certain our son will be blond.

Scanning further down the list, I spot my name. Curious as to its meaning, I read on. 'Ambitious and quick-witted.' I smile and nod. *Fuckin' oath, I am.*

My phone rings, breaking my attention from the name searching. I pick it up and notice Derek's goofy-looking face on my screen. 'Hey, mate. What's goin' on?'

'I was thinking 'bout the intro song for the next gig. How 'bout "Birth" by 30STM?' Derek suggests, apparently forgetting the courtesy of a greeting.

'Yeah, nice! Have you spoken to Will about it? That song has a killer beat.'

'Yeah, Will's on board.'

'Good. I guess we open with "Birth" then,' I reply, still gazing at the list of names on the screen in front of me.

'You busy?'

'No, not really, just looking up baby names.'

'Call the little tacker Derek.'

'Fuck off, dickhead. I'm not calling him Derek.'

'Why? It means "big knob".'

I roll my eyes even though he can't see it. 'Yeah, you can say that again.'

Ignoring my insult, Derek continues. 'He who owns largest cock. Almighty and powerful with massive dong.'

While he's spinning bullshit into my ear, I look up the real meaning of his name. 'You are bloody shittin' me,' I say out loud.

'What? You just looked up my name, didn't you? What's it say? It says big cock, doesn't it?'

'No. It says full of shit,' I answer, closing the subject when really it had said 'the people's ruler'. I'll be damned if I'm going to tell him that, he loves and worships himself enough as it is.

'What did it say? I wanna know.'

'Look it up yourself. Hey, while I've got you, Alexis wanted to know if you and Carly could come round for dinner tonight.'

'I'll check with the missus and get back to you. It should be fine though. Hey, you cookin'?'

I smile at his reference to Carly as his 'missus'. Derek has never been the settling down type. For some reason though, Carly has managed to whip his playboy ways into submission.

'Yeah, I'm cookin'. Ain't I always?'

'I want that pasta stuff you made a while back.'

I know which 'pasta stuff' he is referring to because he helped himself to about four servings. 'No can do. It has ricotta in it. Alexis can't eat that. It could be harmful to the baby.'

'Ah, shit!' he groans.

'I'll do a lasagne. That all right?'

'Done.'

'Good. Talk to Carly and let me know. Dinner is at 6 p.m.'

'Will do, mate.'

We disconnect the call, and I return my attention back to the names in front of me. So far I've jotted down Boyd and Billy. I lean back in my chair and run my hands through my hair, feeling frustrated. *How can you name your son when you haven't seen him yet? What if he doesn't look like a Billy or a Boyd?*

I decide to give up my search for the time being and discuss it with Alexis later ... in bed ... where I hold all the power.

Locking my fingers together behind my head, I smile satisfactorily to myself, now visualising her on the cusp of climax, her orgasm teetering on the very edge, ready to wash over her in sensational waves. The mental picture I now have affords me a sense of total domination, not to mention a stiff dick. Because it's in those moments when she is lying underneath me that she will do and say anything I ask. It's in those moments where I hold the supremacy. Those moments are my favourite form of control.

CHAPTER FIVE

'Mm, that smells delicious,' Alexis moans from behind me as she wraps her arms around my waist.

Just the sound of her moan — whether or not it holds a sexual undertone — stirs my dick within my pants. How she manages to do this to me so often has me perplexed ... but not in a bad way.

'Here, have a taste.' I turn to face her and hold up a spoon containing some of my Bolognese sauce for her to try.

Watching as she gently blows on the spoon through her sweet plump lips, my dick now decides that he too, wants in on some of her blowing action.

She takes the spoon into her mouth, her lips pressing together around the stainless steel implement, and I can't help but watch like it's the most intriguing sight to be seen by anyone, anytime. Suddenly, the lids of her eyes spring apart, and her intently focussed and astonished stare finds mine. Appreciation radiates from her face as I drag the spoon back out of her mouth, deliberately wiping some of the remnants across her lips and chin as I remove it. She raises her hand to wipe my apparently clumsy smear when I gently grab it midair. Our eyes lock, ignite and burn each other with intense passion, love, yearning and lust.

Slowly shaking my head at her and indicating that she not wipe her face, I bring her hand to my lips, pressing a soft kiss on her wrist. She smells like flowers and musk, and her skin delicately caresses my face as I drag my cheek and lips across it.

As I softly place each kiss up the inside of her arm — gradually making my way to my destination — her breathing becomes rapid, her chest rising and falling in short bursts. I notice her eyelids flutter with each press of my lips, together with the subtle shade of pink forming across both of her cheeks.

Smiling with a sense of fulfilment as a man who knows how to satisfy his woman, I let go of her hand as my mouth reaches her neck, nibbling and sucking her most sensitive spots.

'You are so good at that,' she says with praise, as she draws in a ragged breath.

'Honey, I'm fucking good at a lot of things,' I mumble into her skin.

Threading her hands into my hair, she grips it tightly. 'Don't I know it.'

Alexis tugs my head mildly, yet with enough assertiveness to send a searing jolt of wicked excitement right through me and down to my twitching cock. A cock which is aware of its impending duty to stiffen and take form, rubbing the satin of my boxer shorts and hardening against my denim jeans. The now confining space in my pants gives me an increasing urge to unleash my erection and slide it into her warm wet pussy.

I know she's wet; it never takes me long to have her drenched with arousal. *Fuck!*

'Alexis,' I growl, as I push my hips against her and raise my lips to the corner of her mouth. With a quick glide of my tongue, I remove the sauce I deliberately planted there.

She doesn't allow me long to linger at that spot, seizing my mouth with her own in an aggressive, yet passionate attack. We taste each other, suck each other, lick each other and moan one another's name.

Alexis reaches between us and undoes my fly, the sound of the zipper's release assisting my already hardened state. She yanks down my jeans and boxer shorts in one swift move, allowing my cock to spring free with relief, only to be surrounded once again, this time by warm and possessive hands.

Frenzied and visibly hankering, she grips my shaft and then slowly glides both hands up it as though she is praying in thanks for the privilege. Little does she know the privilege is all mine.

'Honey, I fucking love it when you stroke me like that,' I groan into her mouth before licking her bottom lip, teasingly.

She runs her tongue over the spot I have just tasted and pulls away slightly. 'What else do you fucking love me doing to your cock?' she asks, wicked intentions blaring from her.

Alexis is my angel, the most pure light in my life. Yet when I stir sexual desire within her, the sinful, carnal and unashamed amatory devil emerges. I have the best of both worlds and I fucking love it.

'Well?' she asks, her voice saturated in innocence.

The sensation that her hands are applying to my cock renders me momentarily speechless, as if she has cast a spell of lip-paralysing pleasure. I try to respond, but then she sticks her pointer finger in my mouth and caresses my tongue before taking it back out again. I watch eagerly as she reaches back down between us and swirls the now moist digit over the top of my crown. *Jesus fucking*

Christ! 'Tell me, Bryce. Do you like it when I make it wet? Kiss it? Lick it? And suck it?' she asks, the intent behind her eyes unmissable, despite her innocent grin.

'Yes,' I hiss, leaning back against the counter.

Alexis goes to kneel in front of me and, as much as I find it incredibly sexy seeing her on her knees, I can't find it within myself to let her kneel on the floor in her current condition.

I gently stop her by placing my hands on her shoulders. 'Wait!'

'What? What's wrong?'

'I can't have you kneeling on the floor, my love,' I inform her, as I sweep a loose tendril of hair away from her face.

Hoisting myself up on the benchtop, I provide a more comfortable height and position for her to take me in her mouth. 'Better?'

She smiles lovingly at me and steps between my legs, taking hold of my cock once more. 'Aw, such a gentleman,' she drawls.

'Do you like it when I'm a gentleman?'

'Yes ... and sometimes no.'

'What do you want me to be now?'

Smiling seductively, she lowers her head. 'I want to you shut up and let me suck your cock,' she replies, mumbling the last couple of words as she envelops my hard length with her mouth. *Fuck me! She sucks better than a Dyson. I swear all vacuums would bow at her feet if they were aware of her talents.*

Her lips glide up and down my shaft as her hand slowly pumps my base, the building pressure in the head of my dick nothing short of sensational. I love it when she takes me in her mouth, the feelings she elicits with her lips and tongue. But what I love most of all is watching her head bob continuously while her mischievous eyes fuck me, those eyes and the passion within them ruling me completely. Let's face it, it's moments like this that cement the fact I would walk to the ends of the earth for Alexis. Yes, it's only a blow job, but I am a bloke after all and, truth be told, it's a fucking awesome blow job.

She cups my balls, making my cock tighten and my jaw clench, bringing me one step closer to exploding with release. I notice her lips dance a playful smile which makes me instantly aware of what she is about to do, this expression always leading to her favourite move. She tongues the tip of my crown like a lollipop, causing me to jerk uncontrollably. *Bloody hell!*

Just as I'm about to blow, the buzzer to the door sounds. Alexis pauses, looking like a deer in the headlights, except this little doe has a rock-hard cock protruding from her mouth.

'That better not be Santa,' she mumbles around my dick. *Santa? As in Father Christmas?*

'Who's Santa? Apart from the obvious,' I ask.

'Never mind,' she mumbles once more.

The buzzer sounds again, and the look in her eyes asks me what she should do. Sitting and staring at her beautifully compromised face, there's no question what I want. There's no question what any man would want. *Finish me off! Only the inhumane would leave a man on the brink of ejaculation.*

She nods, appearing to nod more to herself than me, and then pumps me vigorously as she sucks with sheer intention. I climb with the building sensation in my dick once again, and this time spill over the edge and into her mouth.

Seconds later I am zipping myself up as the buzzer rings for the third or fourth time, I'm not quite sure. I hand Alexis a tissue, pour her a glass of water and ask if she needs anything else.

'I'm fine. Go answer the door.'

I grab her and kiss her, caressing her beautiful face. 'I fucking love you.'

'Yes, I know,' she smiles, as she gives me a quick peck on the lips and then takes a drink.

Jogging out of the kitchen and toward the entry door, I can't help but grin the satisfied grin of a man well looked after.

'What took you so long?' Derek asks as I open the door to let him and Carly inside. They both stare at me for a couple of seconds as though they want an answer and, just as I'm about to reply with 'None of your fucking business', Derek slaps me on the back. 'On second thoughts, no need to enlighten me,' he says with a cocky grin on his face before walking past me.

'Hey, Bryce,' Carly greets cheerfully, giving me one of her flirty hugs.

I've come to realise that Carly will always be quite willing to allow her hands to linger on my biceps just that little bit longer than necessary. But, I must admit, her level of flirtation has significantly dropped since she hooked up with Derek, this being a good thing. Not only for Derek, but also for my biceps.

'Where's Lexi?'

'Kitchen.' I nod in the direction from where I just came ... *literally*.

Carly smiles and disappears around the corner.

'Speaking of kitchen, smells awesome as usual,' Derek says as he looks around the apartment. 'Wow! This place looks different. Not so much the bachelor pad anymo—'

'You did!' Carly screeches from the kitchen, interrupting our conversation. 'You little whore!'

I furrow my brow. The thought of Alexis being called a whore does not sit well with me, but because it comes from Carly I manage to let it go.

Derek just shakes his head and smiles. 'That girl of mine's mouth needs a filter ... then again ...' he ponders, 'I do love it dirty.'

'I don't want to know about Carly's dirty mouth,' I say with certitude, all the while thinking of Alexis' sweet mouth and the sublime thing she just did with it.

'You just got your dick wet, didn't you?' Derek pokes.

Ignoring the pervert's question, I change the subject. 'Want to see the new recording studio?'

Derek rubs his hands together greedily, dismissing my digression. 'That's what I thought. It doesn't normally take that long for you to answer the door. Plus, you have that I-have-a-happy-cock look on your face.'

I continue to ignore him as we make our way to the recording studio. His reaction to my newly refurbished room will be retribution for his perverted probing.

Opening the door, I wait for it with keen anticipation.

'What the fuck? Dude, this isn't *Playschool*,' he says with a crooked grin on his face and his hands resting on top of his head.

I knew the boys would find the new addition of soft teddies and toy trucks amusing, so I inwardly chuckle to myself. 'No, but when the baby is born, he'll need some toys to play with.'

I walk over to the computer equipment and switch it on.

'Doesn't he have his own toy room? Ya know, other than in our recording space?'

'Of course he does, but I want to spend as much time as I can with him after he's born. They grow so quickly, you know. Look at Alexander. He's already one and a half.'

'I know how old Alexander is,' he grumbles while taking in the new surroundings.

'Look, I don't want to miss a thing if I can help it.'

'I get that. But I don't know, man. Won't it be too loud for him? Baby's ears are kinda small.'

I laugh at the stupid fucker. 'Of course they are small, and anyway, I'm one step ahead of you.' I make my way over to the wicker basket on the floor near the rug and pick up a pair of tiny, fluffy, earmuffs. 'See? It's covered.'

At that moment, Carly and Alexis walk in carrying a couple of beers and wine — Alexis drinking her non-alcoholic rosé.

'This is, um, interesting,' Carly stutters as she takes in the toys.

'You can say that again,' Derek mutters, then turns his back and starts typing on the keyboard.

Scanning the room and its surroundings, I feel proud and excited, knowing my son will — in matter of weeks — be sharing this space. It couldn't be more perfect.

Alexis passes me my beer and stands beside me. 'Yes, I know. I told Bryce that putting toys in here was going a little overboard, but he insisted.'

With my free hand, I slide it behind her back, stopping to rest just above her arse. As always, she snuggles into my side.

'Overboard?' Carly questions a little sarcastically. 'There's a freakin' coloured-ball pit over there. And is that Twister carpet?'

'Sure is. Alexis' idea,' I say proudly before swigging my beer. 'Isn't it great? We have it in many of our family-friendly rooms over in the City Promenade building.'

Carly makes her way over to the colourful spotted carpet. 'It's awesome! I want some.'

'That can be arranged,' I inform.

'I reckon the school would benefit from some as well. Alexis, you could seriously be on to something here.'

I take another swig of my beer and gently caress Alexis' lower back. 'That's what I told her.'

'What? No, it's just a bit of fun.' She dismisses our praise and takes a casual sip of her drink.

'Ah, Bryce, here it is.'

I reluctantly step away from her warmth and walk over to Derek to see what he has found. 'Here's what?'

'Backing music for "Birth". Unless you want to hire a friggin' orchestra and some taiko drums.'

I raise my eyebrow at him.

'Well ... shit, Bryce!' Derek shrugs. 'I never know with you. I wouldn't put it past you to hire the bloody Melbourne Symphony Orchestra.'

'Good on you, I'm not that bad. Backing music is fine. Although I think Will may have a taiko.'

'Sweet! And Luce can handle the electronics on the board. So it's set then, we are opening with "Birth".'

'What else are you going to play?' Alexis asks.

I turn and watch her fiddling with some of the soft toys in the play area, her hand gently caressing a pale blue teddy bear's head. She places it back in the wicker basket then finds my eyes when she realises I haven't answered her question. We have a moment of unspoken words, something we do often, even more so lately than ever before. Right now I'm telling her that she looks fucking beautiful while pondering our son's imminent entry into our lives, and her return stare tells me that she knows what I'm thinking and how I feel about her.

'You two make me gag sometimes,' Carly complains, breaking our silent moment.

'You're just jealous,' Alexis retorts as she closes the gap between us.

'Am not,' Carly mumbles and turns her back to Derek, her face displaying a shade of crimson.

Clearly she is.

Leaning against the pool table, I watch Alexis approach me and drape her arms over my shoulders. My hands automatically find her belly, and I tenderly rub the precious spot.

Ghosting my lips with her own, she asks the question again. 'So, what else are you going to play?'

'What do you want me to play?'

A very subtle moan sounds from the back of her throat; at the same time she delicately licks her lips, lustful desire rolling from her. I love the way my playing the guitar has such a positive affect on her, her reaction always such a turn-on. I must admit though, watching her play the guitar has the same lust-fuelling affect on me too, not to mention the reason why she learned. It still blows me away.

I remember her surprising me, playing at one of our gigs while singing 'The Only Exception'. I was completely stunned, in awe of her capacity to gain this new skill without me even knowing, together with how completely amazing she looked, performed and sang. In that moment, up on that stage, no one except her had existed, her voice having carried a superb musical message which was for my ears only. It was something I would never ever forget, because it was her way of letting me know that no matter what we experienced together in life, we would always pull through.

Since that day, Alexis has been learning more of the basics and is a natural with a guitar. In fact, she is a natural musician. I've given her a few private lessons myself, but the both of us never really get far when I'm teaching; instead we end up on the floor in a sexually charged tangle of body and limbs. Unfortunately, I'm thinking that if she is serious about learning the guitar properly, maybe it's best Derek continues to teach her. After all, he has done a good job so far.

'I'd love to see you all do a Kings of Leon song,' Alexis purrs, bringing me back to the present. She lowers her head and whispers into my ear, her warm breath tickling my lobe. 'You know what their music does to me.'

And there it is, her ability to so easily drive me wild, my cock now wanting out of his pen and into hers. All it took was the sound of her suggestive voice.

'Oh, yeah?' I swallow and grip her tight arse. 'What did you have in mind?'

'"The End",' she says with a salacious smile.

Derek interrupts our moment by singing the first line of the song while playing air guitar like a member of an eighties hair band. Not surprisingly, the talented fucker actually nails the tone and lyrics of the song. Alexis smiles and turns her head toward him, at the same time baring her neck which is only centimetres from my mouth. The smooth, soft skin before me begs to be stroked by my tongue, the fresh floral notes rolling off her, mesmerising me. I lean in and whisper into her ear, 'Do you want me to play it now?'

She turns, her lips just touching mine. 'You know it?'

'I do.'

'Then, yes, Mr Clark, play it for me.'

I push off from the pool table and bend down to kiss her stomach then head for my Gibson ES-137.

Slinging it over my shoulder, I hand Derek the bass and raise my eyebrow at him. 'Lexi wants a quick demo.' I plug the amp in, tune it with a few strums and wait for Derek to count himself in.

As I play my first chord, I take in the sheer worship and adoration in the sparkle of Alexis' eyes. It's one of the best fucking sights imaginable.

***

Later that night in bed, I gently caress her tired body.

'I shouldn't have attempted to play Twister,' she groans.

'Not your brightest idea, my love,' I agree with a smile as I sit up on the bed. 'Where are you sore?'

'My piglets are hurting and my back needs to man-up,' she replies almost sulkily, her gloomy pout so damn cute.

'Here, let me show some love to those piggies.'

'No!' she snaps.

'Alexis, let me rub your bloody feet,' I state, my tone displaying that I'm not in the mood for her objecting to her feet being touched.

She growls then surrenders, placing them on my lap. 'Fine.'

Taking a hold of one foot, I lightly pinch her big toe with my fingers, giving it a gentle wiggle. 'This little piggy went to market ...' I begin.

Knowing she will try to kick me, I quickly secure both her feet tightly, but not tight enough to cause any discomfort. The ankle she broke just over a year ago still gives her a little grief.

'You're mean,' she pouts.

Chuckling, I place a soft kiss on the ankle in question and start to lightly massage the bottom of her foot. 'So, I looked up some baby names —'

'Did you?' she smiles. 'And ... any you like?'

'Nothing that screams "my son". Anyway, how can we name him without seeing him first? The name we pick may not suit him.'

'Pfft, I picked out Nate and Charli's names when I was nine years old.'

I swap her feet, gently placing one down and picking up the other. 'What?'

'Sure did. Jen and I were playing in our cubbyhouse with our dolls. We got to talking about who we were going to marry when we grew up and how many kids we were going to have. That's when I chose those names.'

'You didn't change your mind at all?' I ask, both shocked and a little unconvinced.

Alexis yawns and closes her eyes. 'Nope, I loved those names when I was young and I still love them to this day.'

'What if Rick hadn't liked them?'

She shrugged her shoulders, eyes still closed. 'It would've been stiff shit ... a dealbreaker,' she explains, the corners of her mouth lifting into a smug smile. 'He liked them though, so it was easy really.'

Lightly tickling the side of her arch, I watch her lying there peacefully. 'You are incredibly stubborn, you know.'

'I know someone who gives me a run for my money,' she murmurs.

'So, who did you decide you were going to marry when you grew up?' I ask, curious as to her childhood crush. A sudden dread passes over me, fearing her answer to be Rick. I really don't want to hear that.

'Tom Cruise,' she sighs then opens her eyes and props herself up on her elbows. 'It was because I thought he was a fighter pilot in real life,' she says, while waggling her eyebrows and grinning like the Cheshire cat.

'He's got nothing on me, honey.'

She laughs and drops her head back before bringing it upright again. 'I know, he's not even good enough to be your wingman. So, what names did you look up?'

I screw up my nose, still not overly happy with my results. 'Boyd, which means blond-haired. I figure BB will be blond.' *Fucking BB, she has brainwashed me, I swear.*

'I think that's safe to say,' she smiles. 'What else?'

'Billy.'

'What does Billy mean?'

'I can't remember.'

'So why did you choose it?'

'No reason.'

She narrows her eyes at me, and I can't hide my sly grin.

'Bryce, you're lying.'

'I am not.'

'Yes, you are. Why Billy?'

Realisation spreads across her face 'Oh ... hang on a minute. No way. If you are suggesting Billy because of Billy Brownless, you can forget it. No way is my son going to be named after a Cats player. No way in hell. Pick another name.'

I laugh. She knows me too well. 'You pick one then.'

'Fine. Brayden.'

I repeat the name in my head a few times. *Brayden? Brayden?* The more I say it, the more I like it.

'I was going with Bracken,' she continues, "cause it has all our initials in it, like Bianca did. But I just don't like the sound of Bracken as much as I like Brayden. Plus, Brayden means brave. Bracken means "Bracca's Town" and that's just stupid.'

'Brayden ... I like it. But I still think we need to see if it will suit him first.'

'Whatever,' she huffs happily, while laying back down and closing her eyes. 'I'm telling you, it won't matter. Babies don't look like any name in particular when they are born. They grow into their names.'

I shake my head at her stubbornness once again. 'How do the piglets feel now?'

'Better, thank you.' She yawns again.

'What about a middle name?' I ask.

'I've already picked that one.'

'Is it a deal-breaker?' I probe, playfulness in my voice. *Nothing is a deal-breaker for us where I am concerned.*

'No. But I think you'll approve. At least I hope you will.'

'Uh huh. Well ... what is it?'

She opens one eye and screws up her face, reluctant to answer.

'Tell me. But before you do, if you say Hird or Lloyd or any other Bombers player's name, we will have to forge a deal of the century.'

'Lauchie,' she says softly, her eyes searching mine for approval.

Lauchie ... after my little brother. My heart hammers in my chest and emotion fills my entire body. This woman never ceases to amaze me. Just when I think I can't possibly love her any more than I already do, she does or says something else that has me worshipping her further.

I climb back under the covers and bring her close to me, kissing her lips passionately. 'It's perfect, my love. And so are you.'

CHAPTER SIX

I know I've said this before, but honestly, I love watching Alexis sleep. To stare at her naked back while she dreams, taking in every tiny bit of the beauty she projects during her peaceful slumber. For the past three months, though, she hasn't been able to sleep on her tummy. Therefore it hasn't been the sight of her naked back that I have lovingly absorbed. Instead, I have been privileged with a view of her angelic face and her perfectly rounded stomach — a stomach that makes my heart beat like fuck every time I see it.

Carefully shifting in bed next to her, I make myself more comfortable, supporting my head on my hand and lightly trailing my finger around her protruding belly. My touch is deliberately featherlight, as I don't want to chance waking her; she needs all the sleep she can get.

Last night was exhausting for her, especially after playfully jamming with me and Derek, followed by an awkward attempt at Twister carpet with Carly. If I wasn't mistaken, my best friend — and shameless pervert — found their gently tangled position highly amusing, and not in the funny ha-ha kind of way.

I have no doubt that last night's antics, together with Alexis again having numerous piss-stops throughout each night, is a result of her overtiredness now. Obviously, this is bad for her, but not so much for me. Why? Because I can't help but find her midnight toilet runs entertaining. I know that sounds horrible, but it's true. The grumble of annoyance she makes as she awkwardly rolls and shuffles herself in the bed is fucking adorable. Not to mention her not so hushed cursing of her 'pathetic, weak and sad excuse for a bladder'. It gets me every time. *She's just so funny ... and beautiful ... and adorable ... and fuck ... I'm one lucky son of a bitch!*

Whenever I feel the bed shift during the night, I pry an eye open and smile and wait for the sound of her mumblings before jumping up to help her. I genuinely love helping her, whether it's during the day, evening or middle of the night. Of course she tells me not to and says she can manage on her own, and sometimes she even tries to get out of bed very slowly in order not to wake me. The thing is, it's pretty fucking impossible for her to move without the entire bed moving along with her.

These past few weeks she's repeatedly told me that 'she's over it' and 'thank fuck she's not an elephant' because, apparently, elephants are pregnant — on average — for nearly two years. Don't get me wrong, because I do sympathise with her lack of comfort and sleep, but I can't help finding her frustration over some parts of her pregnancy somewhat comical. *I mean, really, how bad can it be?*

I'm glad I just said that in my head. I'm also glad she is still asleep. Shit! Could you imagine the death stare she would graciously give me if that had, in fact, dribbled out of my mouth?

Obviously, I have no idea what it's like to carry a baby, and I never will — cheers to owning a dick. And while our metaphorical glasses are still raised in a toast to my gender, I think a 'cheers' to my abilities in evading the evil curse known as Couvade Syndrome is also warranted. *Clink!*

Now, seeing as I am the proud owner of a dick, I am left with no choice but to accept that my role during the whole baby-baking process is to acknowledge that everything Alexis complains about is justified: the sore back, the swollen feet, the aching tits and our little precious one practising his soccer skills by bending it like Beckham with Alexis' ribcage. I know when he does this, because Alexis screws up her nose and rubs her abdomen in an annoyed yet nurturing way. It's fucking adorable, and it makes me smile ... which makes her mad ... *really* mad. At the same time though, I do give her my sympathy and jump to her aid, because let's face it, at the end of the day it's the least I can do.

Alexis takes in a sharp breath and her chest rises, pushing out her full luscious tits, taunting me. I'm desperate to press my lips to them, take her soft, perked nipples into my mouth and ravish them with my tongue. *Fuck!* I have a hard-on right now and contemplate trying it, but wonder if I did, would she wake. *Should I? Of course I should.* Then again, her threats of late are becoming quite believable, so a rethink of that course of action is probably wise.

Last week, Alexis made it very clear that her nipples were no longer allowed to find their way into my mouth. She told me they were now 'off limits' because colostrum had appeared. I was no longer allowed to ravish them with my tongue ... well, at least until our son was drinking from a bottle.

Much to my disappointment, I admitted this news did seem fair to me ... until she then told me that he would more than likely start to drink from a bottle when he reached the age of one. *One ... really?*

Fucking bullshit, age one. There's no way in hell I'm waiting that long to suck her nipples. He can drink from a bottle long before his first birthday.

I shake my head at the absurd thought and lean in closer to Alexis' tummy to have a one-on-one discussion with my boy. I do this often, especially when his mother is asleep: secret Daddy business.

'I know you are awake in there,' I whisper. 'I can see you moving around. Listen, you know I love you and will do absolutely anything for you, give you anything you need, right?' I wait for him to acknowledge me with further movement.

He does.

'Good, because I need you to understand that your lease over the use of your mother's nipples is for a term of six months and no longer,' I inform him.

Glancing up at Alexis, I confirm that her eyes are still closed, then return my attention to her stomach. 'You might think the duration of your lease is unfair, but I can tell you I am being very reasonable. So, that being said, do we have a deal, baby boy?' I lightly fist-bump Alexis' tummy. 'Good boy,' I whisper with a satisfied smile on my face and gently nuzzle her skin with my nose. *God, she smells good.*

'I can't believe you just made a deal with our son over his use of my breasts,' Alexis says quite casually without opening her eyes. *Shit! I could've sworn she was still asleep.*

'He needs to know who's boss,' I defensively answer while shuffling closer to her face.

She opens her gorgeous eyes and rolls onto her side, facing me. 'I think you are the one that needs to know who's boss, and I can confirm, Mr Clark, that it is not you,' she says with a contented, cocky grin on her face.

'Honey, you know that is not true. Technically, I am still your boss,' I assert, as I caress her tummy.

She growls, filling me with a devious happiness.

'I need to get up and have a shower,' she adds, now snotty at the truth of my correct words.

I raise my eyebrow at her then get up on my knees, resting back on my heels and giving her full sight of my morning glory. 'A shower ... now? Are you sure?'

'Yes,' she says with a faux yawn, trying to keep her obvious want of me at bay while she begins her practised shuffling to the edge of the bed.

Smiling to myself, I take a hold of my cock and slowly drag my clenched hand along its length, prompting her to swallow heavily.

She stares at me and licks her lips.

I've come to realise over the past year that this action of hers is involuntary. I love it, it reveals her uncontrollable surrender.

'Alexis,' I say, in a low predatory tone as I crawl over her body, stopping her from getting away and placing myself in a spooning position behind her back. 'Are you saying you don't want this?' I ask, continuing to tease her while pressing my cock onto the soft apex of her arse.

Instinctively, she pushes into me, but refuses to look over her shoulder in my direction.

'Uh huh,' she moans, giving me a lazy rub with the rotation of her hips.

I lean forward and lick the skin just below her ear. 'You're lying.'

'I am,' she giggles, then tilts her head back and welcomes my mouth to hers, my tongue to caress her own. *My god, she tastes wonderful.* I could fucking kiss this woman till I run out of breath, and I'm positive there have been moments when I nearly have.

Slowly, I trail my hand down her front and slide two fingers inside her amazing pussy, enjoying the warm wet softness as I penetrate.

'Fuck, Bryce,' she moans, as I swirl them around inside her.

My cock twitches, indicating he too wants a piece of her inner sanctum, so I pull my fingers out and take hold of her thigh, opening her wide and placing her foot on the bed behind my legs. I position the head of my dick at her entrance and slowly push into her. *Jesus, she feels good. How is it that she always feels this fucking good?*

Alexis reaches behind us and grips the back of my head, making me groan and flex my fingers into her hip. *Bloody hell!* I know she likes it controlled and tortuous in the beginning, so I rock my pelvis deeper and harder, but keep my rhythm slow before building my pace.

'Oh, god,' she moans, reassuring me of my thoughts.

Her hand moves away from my head and is transferred to my arse, her nails digging into my now tense cheek — a clear indication of her climbing orgasm.

'I love you so fucking much,' I growl out loud, my momentum picking up with a passionate vigour.

'I love you, too,' she replies breathlessly.

I can never get enough of hearing her say that to me, those three words making me the happiest man alive, my system surging with adrenaline every time.

Moving my cock in and out of her quickly and relentlessly, I feel the pressure start to build in my shaft. She pants heavier now, and her inner muscles clench around me, assisting my release and tipping me over the edge.

'Fuck,' I growl into the crook of her neck, drowning out her cries of gratification.

I trail kisses along the tops of her shoulders and down her arm as I rub out the end of our climax, taking my time and enjoying her body. When both our breathing returns to a normal level, I straddle her lower thighs and hover over her.

'Do you still want your shower?' I say seductively, arrogance in my tone.

'Yes,' she counteracts, 'as a matter of fact I do.'

I chuckle, shake my head, and launch myself off the end of the bed, now primed for the rest of my day. Sex with Lex in the mornin' always has that affect on me.

'Here ...' I reach out my hands as I stand in front of her, offering to pull her up. She accepts and slowly rises to her feet, while letting out an uncomfortable grumble. I'm about to mock her cuteness when suddenly, I feel a warm, wet sensation on the top of my feet. 'What the fuc—'

'Oh, god,' Alexis gasps, letting go of both my hands and clutching her stomach. 'My waters just broke.'

CHAPTER SEVEN

I'm not sure how long I stood glued to that very spot, staring at my wet feet. I'd like to think it was only a split second, but to me it felt like an eternity. Eventually, comprehension of what was occurring right before my eyes smacked me across the face.

'Shit! Shit! Come on,' I go to grab her arm and gently drag her out of the room.

'Bryce, where are you going?' she asks, while pulling against the direction I wish to go.

'To the bloody hospital, where else?'

'I'm naked and so are you.'

I look at her superb, mouthwatering body that transformed into a sexy as hell protective house for our son, then I look at my own bare form. 'Fuck! We need clothes.'

'No shit, Sherlock,' she mocks. 'But I'm having a shower first.'

Alexis casually shrugs out of my grip.

'No. What do you mean? We don't have time.'

She turns and makes her way to the bathroom. 'Yes, we do. It's fine. Anyway, you may want to wash your feet.' *How can she be so bloody calm? Our son is on his way.*

'What?' I say, astounded.

She stops, braces herself against the doorway, then turns back to me and smiles and it is the most hypnotic expression I've ever seen. 'Come on, Daddy. Help me wash. Our baby boy is on his way.'

***

After showering at the speed of light and collecting Alexis' hospital bag, I finally manage to get her in the Crow and on our way to the Royal Women's Hospital.

'Are you okay, honey?'

'Yep, couldn't be better,' she answers sarcastically with a forced smile on her face.

I hold back my laugh.

'Argh! Jesus! Who invented labour pain? Who invented labour full stop?' she whines and pants.

'Are you okay?' I ask again, now concerned at the sudden escalation of her pain.

'Stop asking me that. You'll know if I'm not okay,' she spits through gritted teeth.

Right, mental note: Don't ask if she's okay again.

'We are nearly there, hang on,' I advise tediously, glancing at her from the corner of my eye.

'Hang on? You try hanging on to a baby that wants nothing more than to climb out of your vagina,' she grumbles.

This time I can't help but let out a laugh.

Thankfully, Alexis' phone rings at that same moment, distracting her from the abuse she is about to hurl my way. I'm more than glad to escape her impending vocal bullet and prepare to land the chopper on the helipad as she reaches into her handbag to pull out her phone.

She squints at the screen and blows out long breaths. 'Carls, what's happening?' she answers flippantly through puffs of air.

I smile and shake my head while setting the chopper down and shutting off the engine.

'No, I'm not fucking Bryce,' she explains while pausing for a minute and dropping her head back in amused exasperation. 'I'm not lying,' she pants. 'I'm breathing heavily because I'm in labour, you silly cow. Argh, god! They are getting stronger,' she groans, and for the first time shoots me a nervous look.

'Hang up,' I say calmly.

Alexis nods in agreement. 'Carls, gotta go. I'll talk to you later,' she says breathlessly, as she disconnects the call.

I exit the cockpit and, on my way round to help her out of the chopper, I quickly type Lucy a text.

> Baby on the way. At hospital ~ Bryce

A reply comes through as a nurse pushes a wheelchair in our direction.

> OMG! I will be there as soon as I can ~ Lucy

Sliding one arm behind Alexis' back and the other under her knees, I lift her into my arms and gently place her into the waiting wheelchair. 'Oh, for the love of f-f-frying pans,' she groans.

'That's a new one,' the nurse smiles, before introducing herself. 'We get fire trucks a lot.' *I'm surprised Alexis just doesn't swear. It's never stopped her before.*

'I don't want the f-bomb to be the first word my baby hears coming out of my mouth,' Alexis hisses, breathing out through her teeth as her contraction eases.

The nurse nods. 'That's fair enough, dear,' she says then proceeds to push Alexis toward the birthing suite.

Not even minutes later, Alexis starts cursing again. 'Shit! Shit! Shit!' she groans with puffed cheeks. 'Why? Why am I doing this again? And how did I forget how bloody painful this is?' She glares at me.

Not really knowing how to answer that question — and against my better judgement — I attempt it anyway. 'Because it's worth it, honey,' I say softly, trying to reassure her while patting her hair away from her face.

'Don't pat me like a dog,' she snarls as she swipes my hand away.

Another note to self: don't pat her.

I go to put my hand back in my pocket when she grabs it. 'Sorry ... I'm sorry. I don't mean to bite your head off. It's just ... oh, god! It hurts,' she cries out as she clenches my hand in a death grip. *Jesus fucking Christ, that's hard! When did she get superhuman strength?*

We enter the birthing suite and she lets go of my hand: relief, together with blood flow, returns to my semi-crushed fingers.

'Alexis, dear, my name is Kate. I'm a midwife. Dr Rainer is on her way and will be here shortly, okay? Now, let's get you up onto this bed and check how baby is doing,' she says with a smile.

I help Alexis out of the wheelchair and up onto the bed, assisting her by fluffing up pillows and basically just fucking fluffing about. Obviously, I'm way out of my comfort zone and don't know what the hell I'm doing.

Kate sets up an IV and attaches some straps and cords to Alexis' stomach. 'Now, your hospital chart says you had an emergency C-section with your last delivery. Baby was in breech, right?'

'Yes, yes, she was. Charlotte liked to dance around even before entering this world. Seven years later and she hasn't changed,' Alexis answers lovingly, almost calm and serene.

I gently wipe a bead of sweat that has formed on her brow and take note that even in distress, and obviously a shitload of pain, she is still absolutely gorgeous.

Then, just like a gust of wind, her calm demeanour is swept away and a harsh, boiling disposition replaces it. 'I want an epidural, goddamn it,' Alexis growls through deep breaths while closing her eyes. 'Please!'

Placing my hand on her forehead, I then gently drag my fingers through her hair in the hope of calming her down. *Fuck, she's beautiful.* Her eyes open with lightning speed and she fires a death glare in my direction. *Fuck, she's scary.* Quickly, I panic and lean in to kiss the spot where my hand has just been, apologising for breaking the 'no patting rule'. This seems to do the trick because she smiles meekly at me.

'Your contractions are three minutes apart and lasting just over one minute long,' Kate explains. 'I'm going to check how dilated your cervix is, then we will discuss an epidural.'

Alexis nods.

I nod, too. At this point in time, I think I'll nod at anything being said. Nodding is good.

'Not another one. F-f-fruit cake,' Alexis moans and turns the shade of a tomato. 'I just had one, give me a break.'

I take hold of her hand, remembering not to pat her. 'Just breathe, honey.'

'Seriously?' she huffs.

'That's what you told Lucy to do.'

'I know, but it's bullshit.'

'I just thought —'

'Shut up!'

Another note to self: shut up.

'Bryce I'm sorry. I love you. I just don't like you right now.'

'Yes, you do,' I say with an authoritative tone.

She looks at me with knowing eyes, and mouths with exhausted defeat, 'Yes, I do.'

I bring her hand to my lips. 'I know, honey.'

She nods and closes her eyes during a long exhalation.

Kate positions herself between Alexis' legs, her expression one of concentration. 'Hmm, I'm sorry, dear, but you are nine centimetres dilated so there will be no epidural,' she explains. 'Looks like baby is nearly ready to meet his or her parents,' Kate offers as a compromise, her eyebrow raised persuasively.

'His parents,' I reply, overjoyed. 'We are having a boy.'

'Congratulations!'

'Argh! For the love of f-f-furry freakin' ferrets ... where is Dr Rainer?' Alexis screams, now clearly stressed and in much more pain, not to mention tripling her f-bomb replacements.

'She'll be here any minute,' Kate reassures her, now moving around the room quite quickly and collecting towels, mats, a trolley on wheels with sharp-looking implements that curdle my stomach, and a see-through crib with an overhead light.

Alexis screams out again. 'Fuck! I want to push. I want to push, he's coming.'

'Not yet, Alexis, just breathe through it. You can push in a minute. You're doing really well.'

'What happened to not saying fuck, honey?'

'Fuck you! You try pushing a tennis ball out the eye of your dick and see if you cannot say fuck. Fuck!'

The doors to the birthing suite open, and Dr Rainer walks in with gloves and a big smile on her face. 'Just in time I see,' she says, as she sits on a stool at the end of the bed. 'Bryce, would you like to come and stand next to me and help deliver your son?'

Deliver my son? Me? Are you crazy?

'Sure,' I answer, like it's something I do on a daily basis.

Alexis screams out again and pushes, and all I can see as I stare at her is her mouth moving at a million miles per hour. She looks angry ... and red ... and angry. I can't hear anything she is saying though, because it's like someone has just pushed a mute button and removed all sound. What I can decipher is just how beautiful she is, how amazing and strong she is, and how much I adore her. I smile at her lovingly; she simply takes my breath away.

'Are you smiling at me, Bryce?' she growls, snapping me out of my adoration and removing the silence.

'What?' I stutter.

'I said, are you smiling at me? Does this look fucking funny to you?' she yells.

Mental note yet again: don't smile.

'No. I'm —'

'Okay, Alexis. I see his head. When I say, I want one big push and —'

'Head?' I croak, and take a sneak peek between Alexis' legs. The sight before me nearly has me dying of shock. 'I can see his head, honey. Push!' I command with over-enthusiastic encouragement.

'No. Not yet,' Dr Rainer warns and gives me an annoyed look.

I ignore it.

'No. Don't push,' I add, following her instructions. She is the doctor after all.

'When can I push? I want to push. Screw you all, I'm pushing.'

Dr Rainer places her hands around my son's head. 'Now, Alexis. Push!'

'Now, honey,' I add again.

Alexis lets out a mighty big yell and pushes with everything she has. The sound of her pain and sheer determination rips at my heart, drowning my ears until I hear the most wonderful sound in my life: my son's cry.

Looking down, I see his tiny little body in Dr Rainer's hands, and I can't for the life of me begin to describe what my heart is doing in my chest. I'm stunned, yet so happy, and I want to fucking cry. I never fucking cry.

'Daddy, would you like to cut the umbilical cord?' Dr Rainer says as she hands me a pair of scissors.

I accept them and automatically go on Daddy-autopilot, snipping the cord and helping to wrap him in a blanket. *Shit! He's so bloody small.*

Alexis is now quiet and her breathing is more controlled. Her eyes are wide and damp and her neck is craning up, searching for our boy. Dr Rainer gives him a quick check, then places him on Alexis' chest.

I'm fucking floored, stumped, halted in my tracks. My fiancée is holding our son in her arms and it's the most amazing thing I have ever seen.

'Hi, little boy. It's me, Mummy,' she says as she drags her nose along the bridge of his and kisses his forehead.

Seeing that small loving gesture has my heart thumping like crazy in my chest. 'I love you,' I say softly, finally opening my mouth and finding the words. 'And I love you, too, baby boy.' I lean in to kiss my son for the first time. *Wow!* He's so warm ... and soft ... and perfect. Perfect like his mum.

Sitting on the edge of the bed, I drape my arm around Alexis' shoulder and kiss her like never before. Pouring everything I have into it. 'Thank you. You make me the happiest man alive. Thank you for our son.'

ATTAINMENT

She cups the side of my face, then looks lovingly at the little miracle in her arms. 'So, Daddy, do you think he looks like a Brayden now?'

I gently wiggle his nose with my finger and his lazy little eyes find mine. 'Yes, I do. It suits him.'

She smiles through elated tears and hugs him to her chest. 'Welcome to the world, Brayden Lauchie Clark.'

CHAPTER EIGHT

In the blink of an eye your life can change. How you feel, act, think and see the surrounding world around you. It just changes ... without your say so ... never able to go back to the way it was beforehand. Not that I would EVER want my life to revert back to how it was prior to becoming a father. No way in hell!

Standing here with Brayden sleeping peacefully in my arms and Alexis sleeping soundly beside me in her hospital bed, I feel as if my life has just begun.

I slowly take steps around the room, lightly bouncing and assisting Brayden in a lulled slumber. The swelling on his face is just starting to go down as it is only hours after he entered the world.

'Brayden,' I whisper, while placing a soft kiss on his head, 'Daddy loves you so much and I can't wait to take you home so we can spend every minute together. You and me, buddy, we are going to have so much fun.'

A gentle knock at the door sounds right before it slowly creaks open. Lucy pokes her head around and locks her eyes on me cradling my son. The smile we share in that moment is profound and one only Lucy and I can communicate.

I nod my head and indicate she come in.

As she tiptoes over to where I'm standing, a tear is already making its way down her cheek. 'Oh my god, Bryce, he's amazing!' she whispers as she places her hand on his head and wraps her other arm around my shoulder. 'Congratulations, big bro. I'm so happy for you.'

'Thanks,' is about all I am capable of saying, still semi-speechless from sheer awe.

'It's overwhelming, isn't it? Finally holding, smelling and seeing your baby in the flesh for the first time.'

Staring down at his peaceful little face, I answer. 'There are no words, Luce. No words.'

Lucy nods toward Alexis. 'How is she?'

'Yeah, she's good. Just tired and exhausted, but other than that she's fine.'

'So, it was a quick labour?'

'God, Luce! It was the longest and fastest two hours and fourteen minutes of my life. Alexis though ... well ... she was just simply perfect the whole time. She just ...' I shake my head in veneration as I glance over at her sleeping. 'She just amazes me.'

Lucy gently trails her finger down the side of Brayden's face. 'What did the doctor say about him being four weeks premature?'

'Dr Rainer did a thorough examination after Alexis bonded with him. She was happy with his vitals, and when he attached to feed without a problem, she was even more pleased, saying there was no reason why he couldn't remain in the ward with us.'

'He's a tough little cookie, then, isn't he? Determined and strong-willed already. Hmm, I wonder why that is?' Lucy mocks. 'So, does my gorgeous nephew have a name?'

'Yes, of course he does. It's Brayden ... Brayden Lauchie Clark.'

Lucy is silent for a moment, staring intently at Brayden, her expression full of emotion. She sucks in a deep breath, squeezes my arm, then nods and smiles. 'Perfect, Bryce. He's just perfect.'

'I know.'

'So, have you had anything to eat today? Gone to the loo, that sort of thing?'

'No, not yet,' I answer with contentment, the thought of eating or pissing or anything else not even crossing my mind.

She holds out her arms. 'Okay, pass him over and go and see to yourself.'

As I assess Lucy's outstretched arms, a moment of panic washes over me at the thought of letting Brayden go.

Returning my gaze back to my beautiful little boy, I politely decline. 'No, really, I'm fine.'

'Hey,' she says softly while placing her finger on my jaw to turn my face in her direction. 'It's all right. This is me, your sister. I promise I won't let anything happen to him while you're gone. Just go, take a quick breather, get something to eat and then come back.'

Debating whether or not I should leave him, I reluctantly pass Brayden over to her and, almost instantly, a sensation of loss fills me. Not only are my arms now cold, but I experience a reaction of incompleteness, feeling somewhat unsettled and powerless. *Fuck! Is this what fatherhood feels like? Helpless and vulnerable?*

I lean down and kiss Brayden on the forehead, then check to see that Alexis is still sleeping soundly. 'Okay, but I'm only going for some coffee and the loo. I'll be right back.'

'I'll have a skinny latte, no sugar.'

'Skinny latte,' I mumble to myself as I jog out the door, heading for the cafeteria on the ground level.

***

After what seems like the longest fifteen minutes of my life, I quietly open the door to Alexis' room. Carrying two coffees and a hot white chocolate on a tray, I walk in to find Alexis wide awake and Brayden happily breastfeeding. Lucy is sitting by her bed, pushing buttons on her phone and, it seems, keying in what Alexis is saying.

'Two point seven kilos and forty-seven centimetres long. Born at 11.14 a.m.,' she finishes.

'Thanks,' Lucy offers. 'Nic likes details.'

Alexis looks up as I walk swiftly toward her and Brayden. 'Hey, Daddy, where have you been?'

Worried that she might be disappointed in me for leaving them, I quickly place the drinks on the benchtop by the window and make my way to her side, kissing her forehead and gently stroking Brayden's temple. 'I'm sorry. I didn't mean to leave. I needed —'

'Bryce, it's all right. You can take a few moments to get a drink. We are fine, see? Look, he's such a good feeder.'

I watch him contentedly suckling away and it's one of the single most beautiful sights I've witnessed. Guilt briefly sweeps through me at the thought of telling him to give up his food source after only six months. Alexis' breasts now belong to him and he can have them for as long as he needs.

'I hope you are not planning a reduced leasing term where your agreement with our son is concerned,' Alexis warns.

I chuckle. 'No, honey, I was just thinking quite the opposite.'

'What are you two talking about?' Lucy asks as she gets up and fetches the drinks.

'Nothing,' I advise, wanting my secret Daddy business to remain just that — secret Daddy business.

Passing me my coffee and Alexis her white chocolate, Lucy flippantly responds, 'Fair enough.'

'Now, I've spoken to Mum and Dad, Bryce,' Alexis says as she gently shifts Brayden to feed from her other breast. 'They are on their way here together with Jen. Rick and the kids are also on their way. Jake and Johanna will visit us when we are back at home as Jake is currently on a run to Brisbane. Um ... Carly and Derek are coming in tomorrow for a quick visit. And Tash, Lil, Jade and Steph will also probably visit when we are back at home.'

'Right,' I state, dubiously. 'Alexis, I'm not sure you should have all these visitors so soon. Is it safe for Brayden to have so many people around him? He needs to get stronger first, build up immunity or something. I'm sure I read that somewhere.'

'Visitors are fine, providing they are not sick. I'm sure none of our family and friends would visit if they were under the weather in any way, shape or form.'

I smile half-heartedly at her attempt to ease my mind, all the while thinking that I will now have to go gather some of those surgical masks. The last thing I want is some germy fucker sneezing, or coughing, or even breathing on my baby boy.

Alexis sits Brayden upright and places his tiny head in the palm of her hand, her fingers spreading out on both sides of his cheeks. The position she has him in puffs his already puffy cheeks even more — he looks so bloody cute.

She starts gently patting and rubbing his back. 'Here, do you want to burp him? I need to pee.'

'Sure,' I answer hesitantly, as I sit on the bed.

Replacing her hands with my own as she passes Brayden over, I proceed to mimic what she had just been doing by lightly holding his face and patting his back. He lets out a teeny little burp.

I laugh. 'You get that from Mummy.'

'He does not,' she complains in defence.

'Yes, he does.'

'I burped so much during my pregnancy because of all that hair,' she says as she strokes his fair baby wisps.

'I still don't believe it. Babies having hair cannot make you burp,' I repeat. Although, I must admit, he does have a decent head of hair.

'Yes, they can, Bryce,' Lucy chimes in.

'Thank you, Luce,' Alexis says as she readjusts her breasts and winces.

I notice the obvious discomfort on her face. 'What's wrong?'

'My milk isn't properly "in" yet, so feeding kinda hurts,' she explains. 'Actually, it borders on downright painful.'

Appearing to be in the middle of typing a text message, Lucy adds to the conversation. 'She needs Lansinoh, Bryce.'

'Yes, Miss Know-it-all, I'm fully aware of what Lansinoh is. It's in her bag.'

Lucy pokes her tongue out at me and jumps up. 'I'll get it —'

'No, it's fine. I'll get it,' Alexis interrupts. 'I need to freshen up anyway. I'm going to have a shower.'

'Do you need any help?' I offer.

'No. I'll be fine. I'll yell out if I do.'

I lower my voice so that my smug little sister cannot hear. 'Am I doing this right?' I ask, indicating my method of burping.

Alexis gently brushes her lips across mine. 'Yes, you're doing just fine, Daddy. In fact, you're perfect.'

***

Later that day, I watch Brayden being passed around to person upon person and I really don't like it. I don't fucking like it at all.

First he is handed to Maryann, then Graeme, then Jen. Soon after, he is in Lucy's arms followed by Nic's. Then — of course — Nate and Charli want a cuddle and, as if she hasn't just cuddled him for a good part of the afternoon, Maryann has him once again. Watching what reminds me of a pass the fucking parcel game, I start to get highly irritated, but it's not until he is passed to Rick that I can no longer hold back or bite my tongue.

Seeing Brayden in that fucker's arms makes me feel murderous, bordering on fucking insane and, feeling that at any moment my head will spin around on my shoulders — exorcist-style — I finally put an end to the show and tell.

'Okay,' I voice after a minute or two of Brayden being in Rick's arms — a minute or two of too fucking long, 'I think Mum and baby need a rest. It's been a long day. You are all more than welcome to go back to the hotel and stay. Abigail will make sure you are well looked after.'

I gently pry Brayden from Rick's arms and hold him close, protecting him from any further manhandling. He yawns and starts searching for his food source.

'He's due for a feed anyway,' Alexis announces.

'And his first bath,' a midwife adds, as she enters the room. 'Visiting hours are about to close.'

Straightaway, I like this midwife. This midwife deserves a raise, or a promotion, or an employee of the month award. In fact, I make a mental note to look into offering a personal recommendation for that particular award.

'You heard her,' I speak up. 'Out!'

'But Mum, I want to stay,' Charlotte whines.

'I know Charli-Bear, but you can't. Dad will bring you back tomorrow, won't you, Rick?' Alexis asks with a pleading look on her face.

'Actually,' the midwife speaks up, 'if Dr Rainer is happy with your recovery, there's a good chance you'll be allowed to go home tomorrow.'

'Really, so soon? Oh, that would be wonderful,' Alexis beams, an enormous smile plastering her face.

Strapping a blood pressure cuff to Alexis' arm, the midwife continues: 'I'm not sure that applies to Brayden, though.'

What? I decide this midwife needs a new career, fuck her promotion and award.

Before I can voice my objection to leaving my one-day-old baby boy here alone, Alexis does it for me. 'What? That is absurd. I am not leaving my son here alone. That is not even an option. If he stays, I stay. If I go, he goes. End of fucking story.'

'Alexis! Language,' Maryann scolds.

Jen nudges her mother out of the room. 'Mum, stay out of it.'

'I'll wait outside,' Rick adds. *Good idea, you do that.*

'Ms Blaxlo, I didn't mean you would have to leave him. The hospital has a hotel for mothers who are well enough not to need a hospital bed. Because your son is four weeks premature, he will more than likely need monitoring by a nurse. We need to be sure that he is feeding well and putting on weight before he can go home with you. That being said, Dr Rainer will assess him again tomorrow before a final decision is made. '

'I don't want to stay in the hospital hotel. I don't even want to be in a different room from him.' Alexis looks toward me with an anxious expression on her face.

'The hospital hotel is lovely and is only one building awa—'

'That's not necessary,' I interrupt. Noticing Alexis' heightened distress, I step in to calm the situation down. 'Honey, don't worry. We are not leaving Brayden. I'll sort something out, I promise.'

She nods and glares at the midwife, who quickly prepares Brayden's bath and then leaves the room.

***

Later that night as I lay propped up on my side, Alexis on her side and Brayden fast asleep on the bed in between us, I couldn't possibly be happier. Well ... I could. Alexis is yet to become my wife.

'Shit! I almost forgot,' I proclaim, rolling off the bed and reaching for the baby bag.

Alexis straightens and cranes her neck. 'What? What did you forget?'

'Yours and Brayden's presents,' I answer, holding the two gifts behind my back.

'Presents?'

'Yes. It is Brayden's birthday, is it not?'

'It is. So what did you get him?' Alexis asks, trying to peek around my back.

I reveal one arm and place the soft-knitted guitar next to Brayden, a hugely proud grin covering my face.

Alexis giggles. 'Aw, you got him his first guitar. How adorable.'

'Guitar's aren't adorable, honey. They are cool as shit. Brayden is now the coolest baby in this hospital.'

Laughing, Alexis kisses his forehead. 'Did you hear that, baby boy? You are cool as shit!'

He doesn't respond. He's too cool to respond.

'So, you said presents, as in plural. That means you have something else behind your back.'

Raising my eyebrow at her, I nod.

'Is it for me?' she asks with an excited smile.

'It is.'

'Are you going to give it to me?'

'I am.'

Drawing out the suspense for her — because I know she hates surprises — I slowly reveal my hand, only to put it back out of sight, fooling her. The next second, I have a punch to my bicep.

'All right, all right, here,' I laugh, rubbing my arm and producing the velvet box.

Opening it up for her to see, I watch with anticipation as she goes to put her hand in, then quickly pulls it back.

'I'm not falling for that any more. The box, hand it over,' she demands with a smile.

I laugh and hand her the box. *She knows me too well.*

Alexis opens the box and takes out the gold engraved heart pendant and chain. 'Bryce, it's beautiful,' she whispers as she reads the inscription of all her children's names. A lone tear falls from her eye when she looks up and meets my stare. 'You even had Bianca's name engraved on it.'

I lean forward and wipe the stray tear from her jaw. 'Of course I did.'

'It's perfect, thank you. But I didn't give you anything.'

She tenderly strokes Brayden's face with her finger and gazes adoringly at our son, and I realise it's the single most peaceful and amazing moment in my life thus far.

'Do you really know how much I love you?' I sincerely ask her.

She looks up and smiles. 'Yes.'

'No, I mean do you *really* know how much I love you?'

Her smile softens a little, and she blushes ever so slightly. 'Well, yeah ... I think so.'

'I don't think that you do,' I explain, as I push a lock of her hair behind her ear. 'Today, my life changed and that's all because of you. Today, I received the most precious thing imaginable and again ... that's all because of you. Today, my heart grew beyond all proportions, and you are the reason why. You, Alexis. You have given me something no one else has and ever will. You have given me the best present possible.'

She lifts herself up and over Brayden, then smiles mischievously at me before leaning in to kiss my lips.

'It's what I do, Mr Clark.'

CHAPTER NINE

In the morning that followed, Dr Rainer decided to keep both Alexis and Brayden in hospital an extra day for observation, but then authorised their release the following day after I explained that we were more than happy to have a live-in nurse at the apartment for as long as needed.

She agreed, but felt a midwife would only need to make a few house calls in the week ahead. She was happy that Brayden was already doing exceptionally well, especially now that Alexis' breast milk was — in the words of the Emperor of the Galactic Empire — 'Fully operational'.

Thrilled to finally be taking Brayden home, we made our way out to the underground car park. Not seeing where our car is parked and forgetting to ask Chelsea when she handed me the keys, I lift the remote and click the button. The lights of our brand new Tesla Model S flash, revealing its whereabouts.

'What? ... How? ... When?' Alexis asks, confusion covering her face.

Smiling while holding the hospital bags and many stuffed teddies, I reveal my latest secret surprise. 'This is your new car, my love. It's the safest on the market.'

'But ... I like my Territory, and the Charger and the Lexus.'

I place all the stuff in my arms on the ground next to the navy coloured, high-performance, sports sedan with the best safety rating of any car ever tested. *This car is a wet dream ... with protection.*

'Again, this is the safest car on the market. I want you and the kids as protected as possible.'

She looks as if she is going to argue — and I'm fully prepared to put up a fight — but she refrains, shuts her mouth and just nods. 'Okay, I understand, but what about the chopper? Don't you need to fly it home? And how did you get the car here?'

Shocked by the fact that she didn't argue any further, I quickly pick up the stuff from the ground and place it in the boot. 'Chelsea. She drove the car here this morning then flew the chopper back to the hotel,' I explain while shutting the boot lid.

'Right,' Alexis murmurs, her tone now sounding obviously disgruntled.

I step up to face her and look down at Brayden cradled in her arms. 'Hey, what's the matter? Don't you like the car? I just want you to be safe. I don't ever want to lose anyone I love in a car accident ever again. Please don't fight me on this.'

'I'm not. The car is fine. I'm happy to drive it if it makes you feel better. Honestly, I understand.'

'Then what's the matter?'

'Do I have to spell it out to you?' she sighs.

I really have no idea what she is suddenly upset about, so spelling it out like a first-grade teacher is welcomed.

She searches my eyes then drops her gaze. 'Chelsea.'

'What about Chelsea?'

'I don't trust her.'

'We've been through this, honey. I thought you were okay with her working for us.'

'Us?'

'Yes,' I say firmly. 'Us.'

'That doesn't mean I have to be all cheery when you mention her name. I still don't like the bitch,' she spits out.

Shit! Where the hell has this come from all of a sudden? I'm taken aback by her vehement and unexpected insecurity. Maybe this is part of the 'baby blues' thing that the midwife mentioned. Or maybe it could be the start of postnatal depression.

Worried that it could lead to something quite serious, I make a mental note to ring Jessica when we get home.

'Alexis, I really don't want to argue about Chelsea with you. She is no more than a friend, an employee. Look, I don't want to argue with you at all, especially here … now … in the car park on the day we bring our baby boy home for the first time,' I say as I gently drag my knuckle down her cheek.

She gives me one of her faux smiles, places Brayden in my arms and turns for the car. 'Neither do I.'

***

Soon after we arrived home from the hospital, I realised that I wanted Brayden close by pretty much all the time. It had been less than twenty-four hours when I'd decided the solution to my predicament was to order more bassinets, one to be placed in the lounge area and the other in my office. Charli had asked for one to be put in her room as well, which I thought was cute. However, Alexis had felt I was going 'overboard' and soon put a stop to any more of my baby furniture purchases.

The kids had been wonderful, adjusting really well to having a new sibling. For the first couple of days, Charlotte had followed Alexis around like a bad smell, wanting to know every single tiny detail about her baby brother. Needless to say, I was impressed with her inquisitiveness — she was good at creepy research.

Nate, on the other hand, had been a little quiet at first and this had worried both Alexis and me. It wasn't until we started giving him special responsibilities, like making sure his Mum had a glass of water every time she was feeding, and helping me to bath Brayden, that he soon resembled his normal self again.

***

Currently inundated with work, I have no choice but to spend a lot of my time in the office. However, due to my additional bassinet purchase at the beginning of the week, Brayden can spend some of that time with me. It's a win-win situation.

'Bryce, you can't take him with you everywhere. A little separation is good, you know,' Alexis says with her arms crossed while standing at the door to my office.

I glance down into his bassinet which is next to my desk. How separation can be good for someone, let alone a newborn baby, baffles me.

'You are creating a rod for your back. Actually, you are creating a rod for my back,' she grumbles. *What?*

'What are you talking about?' I ask with a smile, her frustration mildly cute. The only rod I create is the one in my pants, which is also the one I currently want in between her legs.

'It means that what you are doing now will create problems in the future. If you continue to take him everywhere with you, it is what he will get used to and he'll want it all the time.'

I take in her form as she leans into the doorjamb. She has on a pair of yoga pants and a tight fitting t-shirt. Her baby bump is almost non-existent and her hair is in a ponytail dangling down her back, longer than it ever has been. She looks stunning as per usual.

'What's wrong with wanting that?'

'Argh!' she groans. 'You just don't get it.' *Fuck, that groan. I love that fucking groan.*

I feel like baiting her more just to hear that groan, because apparently I will have to wait a couple more weeks before I can hear it as a result of my making love to her.

'I do get it. And he's fine. He's barely a week old. He needs to know his daddy is always close. I don't want him thinking any other way.'

Her attempt to hide her grin fails as she runs her tongue over the top row of her teeth.

Just as I'm about to get up and make my way over to her to run *my* tongue over her teeth, my phone rings.

I press speaker.

'Yes.'

'Hi, Bryce, it's Chelsea. I need to make an appointment with you for later today in order to discuss the flight transfers for VIP guests at next week's AFL Grand Final. Do you have time?'

I look in my diary which is as confusing as fuck. I desperately need to get Lucy on it. 'I have some time at 3 p.m. I can see you then.'

'Looking forward to it.'

Aggravated by how disorganised my schedule is, I quickly dismiss her. 'Okay, I'll see you then.'

I hit the disconnect button on the phone and take a deep breath before looking up, suddenly remembering that before I was interrupted, I was about to taste the mother of my son.

Finding the doorway vacant, I screw up my face. I wonder where the fuck she has gone when I spot movement from the corner of my eye. Turning to the window to look onto the balcony, I find Alexis working out on the gym equipment — working out probably an understatement. She is going hard and clearly in a determined mood. *Jesus! Why is she always so fucking determined to try death by exercise?*

I pick up Brayden and walk into the lounge area to transfer him to the bassinet beside the piano. *See? Multiple bassinets ... fucking genius.*

I make sure he is still sleeping soundly before heading to the balcony. 'You might want to take it easy,' I state, a little annoyed that I have to remind Alexis once more to tone down her over-exuberant fitness training.

'Don't start this shit with me again,' she snaps. 'I'm no longer pregnant and am now fully capable of working out.'

'Alexis, I'm just saying that you gave birth a week ago. Your body is still healing and adjusting. Don't rush things.'

'I'm not.'

I notice her refusal to look at me, and it reinforces the concern I felt the morning we brought Brayden home, the morning I mentioned Chelsea.

Curious, I decide to pose that question. 'Has this got anything to do with the fact Chelsea just rang?'

Alexis presses a button, accelerating her strides on the treadmill. 'No. The flying fuck I give about that bitch just flew the fuck away,' she says sarcastically while flapping her hands like a bird.

Really? Clearly that is not the case.

'Honey, why does she make you so angry?'

'Because.'

'Because is not an answer. Alexis, talk to me.'

'No, go away.'

Bloody hell! I want nothing more than to carry her kicking and screaming up to the bedroom and force her to talk to me while my cock is planted firmly in her pussy. But I can't. That form of dominance is a no-go at the moment and it pisses me off.

Having no other choice, I reach into my pocket, take out my phone, and dial Jessica. She answers after only a couple of rings. 'Bryce, dear. How's fatherhood treating you?'

'Hello, Jessica,' I state, while watching Alexis' reaction. 'Fatherhood is wonderful. Perfect, in fact.'

Alexis closes her eyes briefly and sucks in a long, deep breath.

'Lovely. How can I help you? We are not scheduled for a session until Thursday. Do you need to see me earlier?' Jessica asks, hope in her voice.'

'Actually, yes. I would like you to come over today, if possible.'

'I can organise that. Is everything all right?'

'Well, I'll leave that up to you to decide. Alexis is ... let's just say, displaying signs of angry frustration. She won't talk to me about it, so I'm a little concerned.'

'Oh ... you didn't just go there,' Alexis hisses, her fiery glare incinerating me on the spot.

I glare back at her, determined to sort this shit out. I'm not having one of the happiest times of our life marred by her pent-up, unwarranted feelings of jealousy toward Chelsea.

'Okay, I can be there in an hour,' Jessica informs.

'Thank you. See you soon.'

I end the call and put the phone back in my pocket, my stare never wavering from Alexis.

She accelerates her strides even more, practically punching the button with her clenched fist. 'I can't believe you just insinuated I am not coping well after giving birth. Firstly, you have no right. Secondly, I am dealing with mothering our gorgeous son just fine, thank you very much. To even imply that I cannot handle him or —'

'I'm not implying that at all.'

'Then what was that?'

'You need to talk about whatever it is that is pissing you off. And if you won't talk to me about it, you can talk to Jessica. You should be exceedingly happy at the moment, but you aren't. I don't want you to look back at this time and have any regrets.'

She hits the emergency stop button on the treadmill and comes to a halt, slumping over the armrests. Taking deep breaths and looking somewhat exhausted, she wipes her brow with a towel.

After a few seconds of catching her breath and getting her bearings, she steps off, grabs her water bottle and has a long drink before walking up to me. 'I have no regrets ... none at all, none where you and Brayden are concerned. I never have and I never will,' she says quietly, hurt evident in her voice.

I watch her walk back inside before stopping at the bassinet and smiling at our son. The love she projects for him is obviously genuine and in abundance which just confuses me all the more. *Then why is she so unhappy all of a sudden?* I sigh and pray that Jessica will figure it out.

***

Just over an hour later, I let Jessica into the apartment.

'I like what you've done with the place,' she says admiringly, grinning at the now babyfied surroundings.

'Yeah, feels more like a home now.'

'So, where is she?'

'Up in our room with Brayden. Just go straight up.'

'You sure? I don't want to start a session with an already irate patient. It's much more work on my part.'

'It's fine, she's feeding. I'm sure she won't mind.'

Jessica winks and squeezes my arm before giving me a tight embrace. 'Congratulations, I'm so proud of you. And don't worry, I'll get to the bottom of whatever is bothering Alexis.'

'Thank you,' I reply while watching her make her way up the stairs before I head for my office.

As I sit down, I'm instantly made aware that the baby monitor on my desk is switched on as I hear the sound of Alexis' voice singing 'Baby Mine'. As her words filter through the small portable speaker in front of me, I am transfixed by the indisputable love she projects as she sings them. I could sit here forever and listen to her heartfelt words to our son. It's mesmerising.

'Excuse me, Alexis. Sorry, am I interrupting you?' Jessica says, her voice also now sounding through the speaker.

I go to switch the baby monitor off, but pause with my hand on the button, unable to bring myself to do it. It's my excessive curiosity and basically having to know every single detail which prevents me from doing so. Instead — as my conscience goes to war with itself — I sit and continue to listen.

'No, that's all right. I'm just settling him for sleep,' Alexis informs.

There's a pause for a moment and I hear some muffled sounds.

'Oh, goodness, he is just a perfect little angel,' Jessica coos.

'Isn't he just? Here, would you like a cuddle?'

'Do you not want to put him down to sleep?'

'It's fine. He basically lives in Bryce's arms, so he's used to it.'

'Well, in that case, I'd love to.'

There's another pause in discussion and some more muffled sounds.

'My, oh my, does he look like his father.'

I hear Alexis giggle. 'Yes, he sure does.'

This statement has me grinning from ear to ear when my phone rings. Annoyed by the interruption, I buzz Abigail. 'Abigail, can you please hold all my calls until further notice.'

'Certainly, Mr Clark,' she responds, the ringing ceasing immediately.

'Thank you.'

I hang up and continue to listen to the monitor.

'So how's everything going? Is he feeding well? Are you getting enough sleep?' Jessica asks.

'Now, Jessica ... you wouldn't be here to find out if I'm suffering postnatal depression at all, would you?' Alexis asks with a playful tone to her voice.

Jessica laughs and it has me a little perplexed. That is exactly why she is here.

'No, Alexis. Well, that is why Bryce asked me here. But no, I just wanted to see your handsome and incredibly adorable little son.' *Traitor! Fucking traitor!*

I'm just about to get up from my desk and march upstairs to demand she put her skills — that I pay a considerable sum for — to use, when she continues speaking.

'However, since I am here, and seeing how you are clearly not suffering from postnatal depression, do you want to tell me why Bryce is so concerned? Obviously you have given him reason to be.'

Clever woman, why did I doubt her?

'It's my own insecurities, Jessica,' Alexis sighs. 'I'll get over them.'

'Insecurities about what? You look great. You're healthy, you're —'

'I look great? Pfft, I have a long way to go to get back to the weight I was happy with. The weight I was when I met Bryce.'

She has a long way to go? Fucking bullshit! She looks as stunning as ever.

'Alexis, I'm not going to stand here and tell you that these insecurities about your post-baby body are ridiculous, because they are not. Nearly every mother to have just given birth feels this way. It's quite normal. What I will say, though, is give yourself a break. You will get back to the weight you want to be, in time.'

'I may not have time,' Alexis mumbles, so softly that I can barely hear.

'What do you mean?'

'Nothing, it's nothing. Look, I know I will never be a skinny supermodel and I never want to be. I was happy with my curves and being a size twelve. After all, I am thirty-seven years of age and a mother of three. It's just ... I want to get back to that weight as soon as possible. I don't want to risk —'

Alexis cuts herself off.

'You don't want to risk what, Alexis?'

Leaning in closer to the monitor, I strain to hear what she is so worried about.

'I don't want to risk losing Bryce,' she says sadly.

What. The. Fuck? *Lose me? Why would she lose me? She will NEVER lose me!* With my heart hammering in my chest, confusion plagues me as to why she would feel this way. As far as I am aware,

I have never given her cause to believe I would abandon her. It doesn't make sense to me.

'Alexis, why do you feel you could lose Bryce?' *Yes, why?*

'Because it's happened before,' she exclaims, her voice now raised and sounding desperately troubled. 'After giving birth to Charlotte, I waited too long to lose my baby weight and Rick ... well ... he obviously didn't find me attractive any more and went elsewhere. He had an affair with a younger, slimmer, prettier woman. God, Jessica, I don't think I'd cope if Bryce does the same. It will kill me. I can't let that happen. I won't let that happen. I won't let Chelsea take him away from me,' she shouts, desperation in her voice.

Fuck! Fuck me! The pieces start to fit together.

Brayden's little cry sounds through the monitor.

'Oh, baby boy, Mummy is sorry. I didn't mean to frighten you,' she sobs. 'God, I'm so sorry.'

I hear another muffled sound together with Alexis sobbing in the background and it tears me apart. I want nothing more than to run to her and comfort her, to let her know I would never do what Rick did. EVER! And, I want to kick his fucking head in for making her feel this way.

'Alexis, Bryce is not your ex-husband.' *You can say that again.* 'He is undeniably in love with you and I can confidently say would never betray you like that. You need to trust him, but first and foremost you need to trust in yourself.'

'I do trust him. I just don't trust Chelsea. She made it very clear to me after we lost Bianca that she was in love with him. I warned her then to back off, but I know women like her; they wait like a snake in the grass. Wait for their time to strike. And she's fucking waiting, I can tell.'

I run my hands through my hair, completely dumbfounded by what I am hearing. *Am I that oblivious to Chelsea's feelings? Does she only have eyes for me? Shit!* If that is the case, no wonder Alexis is acting the way she is.

'Maybe you should tell Bryce how you feel,' Jessica suggests. 'He has known Chelsea for a long time and is probably unaware of her true character. In fact, I can assure you that he is unaware of her true character.'

Alexis sighs. 'I don't think it will matter, Jessica. Where Chelsea is concerned he is like a brick wall.'

What? Am I?

'Okay, well in that case we work on you by making you feel better about yourself. We need to build up your confidence, starting with a trip to the hairdresser. I think you should organise a girly pampering afternoon with your friends.'

'That's actually a great idea, but what about Brayden? I can't exactly take him with me.'

'I think his father will cope.'

'Oh, I know that. Bryce has been an exceptional dad so far. He's perfect. I have no qualms there. It's just, he is so busy.'

'I'm sure he'll be fine. Call Lucy in if it makes you feel better. Or speak to Arthur.'

'No. I'm not going behind Bryce's back and interfering with his business. No way in hell. That is his domain.'

Brayden's little cry pierces through the monitor again.

'Is he ready for a feed?' Jessica asks. 'I'll let you get back to it then.'

'He shouldn't be, the little guzzle-guts. But thank you. Thank you for coming and talking to me.'

'Anytime, dear. And remember what I said. Bryce is not Rick.'

'I know. I just ... I get a bad feeling about Chelsea.'

'I can see that. If talking to Bryce about it is off the cards, take matters into your own hands and build your confidence back to the level it should be.'

'I will, Jessica. Thank you.'

Brayden cries out again, except this time he is letting Alexis know he wants a feed.

'All right, hungry little piggy, I'll get them out for you. God, you are so much like your father.'

I laugh. Yes, he is like me, wanting to latch onto her nipples every chance he gets. Except that I want to for a completely different reason.

'I'll let myself out. Take care, and contact me if you need anything,' Jessica says as her voice trails off into the distance.

'Thanks, I will,' Alexis calls out.

Seconds later I hear what sounds like Alexis unclipping her bra, and then that unmistakable sound of Brayden suckling. I'm totally jealous.

'Whoa, settle petal,' she giggles. 'There's plenty of milk in there and it's all for you, buddy. No need to try and rip Mummy's nipple apart to get it.'

Loving to eavesdrop on their time together, but at the same time wishing I could see them both, I consider looking into a video monitor when I hear a knock on my office door. Knowing that it's Jessica coming to say goodbye, I quickly switch off the monitor and call for her to come in.

I play dumb as she walks toward me. 'How did you go?'

'Just fine, Bryce. She is definitely not suffering from postnatal depression.'

I nod and smile. 'That's great. So, what is the matter?'

'I can't tell you, you know that. But what I can tell you is this: open your bloody eyes, especially where certain members of your staff are concerned. And pay her attention. Tell her how much you love her. Tell her how incredible she is and, most importantly, tell her how incredible she looks.'

I continue to nod and smile. Her requests are second nature to me; making Alexis feel good about herself is one of my favourite pastimes. 'I will,' I promise.

'Good. Call me if you need me. And by the way, Brayden is superb,' she states, smiling brightly. 'If ever you need a babysitter, you know where I am.'

'Noted,' I say as she approaches the door and lets herself out.

Once Jessica is gone, I start to think about everything I overheard. Alexis' need to get back to her pre-baby weight. The fear she has of losing me. That fuckwit ex-husband of hers and how he has destroyed her confidence. And her thoughts on Chelsea's true character.

Swivelling my chair to face the view of Port Phillip Bay, I take in the scenic vision that has many times granted me clarity in determining a course of action. This time is no different from before as I decide what my next step will be. A step that involves planting a seed, and we all know how much I love gardening.'

CHAPTER TEN

'You're beautiful, you know,' I say as I break the silence while watching Alexis feed Brayden. 'And I love you more than life itself. That will never change.' I walk into the room and sit next to them, picking up the soft guitar and nervously fiddling with it. I don't know why I'm so nervous. I guess I just don't want her to be angry with me any more. I feel like a complete arsehole.

Alexis gives me a critical look. 'Did Jessica speak to you?'

'No, not really. She just assured me that you weren't suffering from postnatal depression.'

She stands up and walks over to the nappy change table. 'I told you I wasn't.'

'I know you did. But I had to be sure.' I put down the guitar, wanting to help her, wanting to make things right. 'Here,' I say, stepping up next to her, 'let me.'

She moves aside and allows me to take her place.

'Hello, Daddy's boy,' I coo like an idiot, something I have absolutely no control over. Even when I try desperately not to talk to my son using my daddy-baby voice, it still comes out of my mouth that way. God only knows how much shit Derek and the boys are going to pile on me when they hear. 'Let's change this wet nappy and get you all clean and dry, yeah?'

I open the nappy to find the filthiest-looking mushy substance known to man. Fuck, I can't even begin to describe what colour it is.

After wiping his dirty arse and sliding a clean nappy underneath — just like Alexis showed me — I hold out the folded nappy-of-death for Alexis to dispose of.

I then lift Brayden's bottom to position him correctly and wipe his little fella clean. Just as I am about to secure the clean nappy, a fountain of yellow baby piss hits me square in the face.

What. The. Fuck?

I hear Alexis muffle her mouth with her hand and, even though my eyes are closed and painted with urine, I know she is about to burst into laughter.

'Did our son just piss in my face?' I state calmly.

Alexis, still trying desperately to stifle her outburst, croakily responds. 'Um ... yes, yes, he did.'

'Right. Do you want to hand me a towel, or a wipe, or a fucking tissue?' I ask, still keeping my tone calm.

'Sure.' She lets go of her bottled outburst and cracks up laughing. 'I would love to.'

Seconds later I feel her wiping Brayden's piss from my eyes, followed by my lips and the rest of my face. And, now feeling that it is safe to unseal them, I pry one eye open at a time to find one happy little boy squirming around underneath my hand.

'You think that's funny, don't you?' I ask him. 'Pissing on daddy like that.'

'You need to keep his Mr Doodle covered with either the nappy or a towel AT ALL TIMES!' Alexis reaffirms as she leans down and kisses Brayden's head. 'Otherwise this little cheeky critter will give you a golden shower. Won't you?'

'Speaking of shower, that's where I am headed now,' I declare as I walk toward the en suite.

'Bye, Daddy,' Alexis calls out from behind. I turn around to find her holding Brayden and waving his little hand at me. 'Thanks for changing my nappy.'

'You're welcome, baby boy,' I reply with a laugh. 'Anytime.'

***

After a quick shower, I discover it is almost time for my appointment with Chelsea. As I make my way down the stairs, I find Alexis sitting on the floor with Brayden lying on a bunny rug beside her. She is holding a brightly-coloured caterpillar-looking thing not too far from his face.

'Boo!' she coos at him, after pulling it away quickly. 'I can't wait for you to smile for the first time, BB. Something tells me you will have a smile like your daddy.'

BB? I thought we dealt with that shit.

I quietly and purposely walk up behind them. 'BB?' I question, while firing an interrogative expression her way.

She startles a little and looks up with an uh-oh, I-just-got-busted look. 'Um ... yes! Baby Brayden.'

Realisation dawns on me. 'That is why you wanted the initial B, isn't it?' I ask, impressed.

She giggles, revealing her plan. 'Maybe.'

'You never cease to amaze me,' I say, shaking my head with a smile. 'Listen, I have my appointment with Chelsea now. I want you and Brayden to come in to the office while she's here.'

'I really don't want to,' Alexis murmurs without looking at me. 'We are happy here.'

The buzzer to my office sounds and we both look at the speaker. Why we do this I'm not really sure.

'Please, I want to show off my son ... and the amazing woman who gave him to me.'

I hear her make a 'pfft' noise, and her confident demeanour from seconds ago is now gone. It saddens me.

'Sure, if it means that much to you,' she says with clear distaste, as she slowly gets up from the ground and takes Brayden to my office.

I'm ready to put Alexis' and Jessica's theory to the test. Surely Chelsea isn't as bad as they say she is.

***

Heading to the door I open it to find Chelsea seated in reception, brushing down her dress and fixing her hair and makeup. Instantly, I pick up on her effort to make herself presentable. Normally, I would find this preparation an honourable quality, something that employees or business associates should make a habit of doing before a meeting. This time, though, I see it more as an attempt to impress me on a different level.

My new-found insight surprises me.

'Good afternoon, Chelsea. Please come in.' I stand back and hold the office door open for her, remembering what my mother had always said about being a gentleman: 'Chivalry is only dead if you yourself kill it.'

Expecting her to walk in like I directed her to, I'm shocked when she stops and places a quick kiss on my cheek. 'Hi, it's nice to see you again. I feel we haven't caught up in such a long time.'

Okay, that kiss was unprofessional and certainly not called for, considering my fiancée is in the room and has just recently given birth to our son.

Worried because this particular experiment is now proving Alexis and Jessica's theory correct, I quickly give Alexis a glance to check I haven't upset her any further. I honestly did not see Chelsea as this brazen before now. *Shit! Have I been that blind?* I expect to see Alexis resembling a cartoon character with steam billowing out of her ears and nostrils. Instead, I see a withdrawn woman who is extremely uncomfortable.

Chelsea follows my line of sight toward Alexis. 'Oh, hello, Alexis. I didn't know you would be here,' she says with a sweet, but somewhat bitter, tone of voice.

'Well, I do live and work here, Chelsea,' Alexis replies, just as bitterly sweet, while cradling Brayden in her arms, 'and this is my fiancé's office, so I'm bound to be around, aren't I?'

'Yes, you are,' Chelsea replies curtly. She looks back at me, waiting for my instruction as to where we should sit.

Thinking that she would have acknowledged Brayden by this stage and be asking how he is — heck, even asking what his name is — I'm surprised that she hasn't. *Maybe it's because he is in Alexis' arms and approaching her would be awkward due to their obvious animosity toward each other.*

I decide to put that theory to the test, too, and take Brayden from Alexis. 'Chelsea, this is Brayden, Alexis' and my son,' I say proudly, stepping up right beside her.

'He's cute,' she replies, giving him a quick smile, then focussing back on me. 'But then again, he is your son.'

I furrow my brow, her flirting obvious and quite frankly pathetic.

At this point, I'm pissed off. Pissed off because, one: I've been so fucking blind and, because of that, Alexis has been hurt, and, two: I fucking hate it when I'm wrong. And, three: the way she just treated my fiancée and son in front of me was nothing short of appalling.

Moving away from Chelsea, I pass Brayden back to Alexis and kiss her with a purposeful show. When I'm done, I turn back around and ask Chelsea to sit in the seat in front of my desk. She does, but not before shooting Alexis a subtle scowl.

Sitting down opposite her, I steeple my hands in front of me and prepare myself to potentially lose an old friend. 'Chelsea, I'm going to have to let you go,' I say neutrally.

'Let me go wher—'

'Your behaviour, especially today in this office, is unprofessional and quite frankly embarrassing. I made it exceedingly clear that we were nothing more than friends a long time ago, and I'd honestly hoped you could work here with a proficient, friendly and skilled manner. Clearly, you can't. And that being the case, I'm sorry to say that your employment with Clark Incorporated is now effectively terminated.'

Chelsea sits stunned, mouth agape, searching my eyes for some form of reprieve or indication that what I just said was some strange ploy. Slowly, she turns to face Alexis. 'You. This is all your doing.'

I stand up and gesture that she do the same. 'I can assure you that this has absolutely nothing to do with Alexis. I had every intention of giving you the benefit of the doubt today, truly sceptical that what I had suspected was just that: an unwarranted suspicion. Unfortunately, Chelsea, you have proved me wrong, and because of that and the way you feel, I can't have you working here any more. It's not fair to Alexis and it's not fair to you.'

Chelsea stands up, fury and hurt in her eyes. 'And how exactly do you think I feel, Bryce?'

Seeing the hurt seep out of her is unsettling, and the last thing I want is for her to be upset, but I now realise she needs to be told bluntly, once and for all, that she holds nothing more than my friendship.

'I think it's obvious how you feel. Can you honestly stand there and tell me that you don't have feelings for me, Chelsea? That you haven't harboured those feelings since we hooked up all those years ago,' I candidly request.

She looks down at her hands, her bottom lip trembling. 'I can't.'

'And that's why you have to leave. Move on. You can't do that here.'

She nods slowly, but doesn't look up.

'Listen, I want you to be happy like I am. Find that special someone you deserve to have in your life ... because that someone is not me. I belong to Alexis and I always will. We have a family and we will be married in the near future.'

She looks up at this point and finds Alexis and Brayden. I find them too, taking in Alexis' tear-streaked face.

Chelsea sucks in a breath and covers her mouth with her hand. 'I'm sorry, Bryce. I ... I just thought that we ...' She momentarily shuts her eyes and shakes her head. 'You're right, I've acted terribly. God, I need to leave. Shit! I'm sorry.'

She turns and heads for the door with rapid speed. I take a step forward, my intention to chase her down. I don't want her to leave in the state she is in. Hesitating for a mere second, I pause, fearing that if I do go after her, I will give her the wrong impression.

Alexis hands me Brayden. 'Here, take BB. I'll go after her.'

I watch her run off, wiping her eyes.

Minutes later, Alexis walks back into my office. I've already placed Brayden down in his bassinet, and he is — as per usual — fast asleep.

Standing up from my seated position behind the desk, I make my way around to the front of it and lean my arse against the edge. 'How is she?' I ask, worried about the answer.

'Devastated —'

'Shit!' I run my hands through my hair in frustration. I really didn't want it to end this badly.

Alexis steps up to me and takes my hands in hers. 'Devastated ... but she'll be okay. You gave her the wake-up call she needed.'

Letting go of her hands and placing mine on her hips, I guide her closer and press my mouth to hers, the taste and feel of her body instantly healing my apprehension.

'Believe it or not,' she whispers, pulling away from my mouth, the loss of her tongue agonising, 'you did her a favour.'

I rest my forehead on hers and momentarily close my eyes. 'I know. But I feel terrible.'

'That's because you have a big heart.'

'A heart that belongs to you and only you. I wish you would realise that.'

'I do ... now.'

She tilts her head up to kiss me once again, and I welcome the invitation eagerly. No one makes me feel what Alexis makes me feel. No one ever has. It's as though we are two kindred spirits; two halves of a whole.

'Jessica told you, didn't she? You won't confess because if you do you admit she broke patient-client confidentiality. I get that.'

'No, she didn't,' I admit sheepishly. 'I heard your entire conversation through the baby monitor.'

Still secured in my arms, she leans backward and looks at the monitor, then back to me. 'Did you not think to switch it off?'

'I was going to, but when you started talking about being afraid of losing me because of what Rick did, I just had to listen. Honey, I would never, EVER, do what Rick did to you.'

A tear falls from her eye, slowly sliding down her cheek. I stop its descent as it reaches her jaw and place a kiss where it had been only seconds ago. It kills me to think that what Rick did shortly after Alexis gave birth to Charlotte has resulted in a lack of faith in herself. *Fuck! I want kill the arsehole.*

'You, my love, are perfect in every way,' I say, kneeling down before her. I lift her top, bunching it just under her breasts. 'Every. Single. Bit of you,' I reiterate in between placing kisses along her stomach.

'Even this new stretchmark here?' she asks, pointing to the pale pink scar on her tummy.

I drag my tongue along it and watch her close her eyes, not sure at this point if they are closed due to discomfort or pleasure. 'Especially this one, because this one signifies what you endured to give me the most precious gift imaginable.'

CHAPTER ELEVEN

A few weeks after we jumped Alexis' Chelsea-hurdle, Alexis is nearly back to her old self. I couldn't be happier. She has been hitting the gym quite hard though, and as much as I don't like seeing her treat her body so harshly I figure it's best to stay out of it. I don't want to dampen her improving mood.

Standing at the window in my office, looking onto the balcony where she is now using the weight machine, my dick throbs in anticipatory agony. I'm almost at the point of having to go knock the top off it just to get some relief. I desperately want to be inside her, having not made love to her for nearly four weeks due to her post-birth healing.

I suck in a breath and growl like a friggin' bear as I watch her legs open and close, her abductor muscles flexing and taunting me. Right now I wish they were closing and clenching around my head while I taste her sweet pussy, followed by them tightening and clamping around my hips as I fuck her senseless. *Jesus, fucking Christ!*

Adjusting my raging hard-on, I shuffle to get some relief, but my relief is short-lived. She stands up, then grabs her towel and bottle of water and I watch with perverted delight as she drags the towel across her forehead, over her face and down her neck. I've never wanted to be a towel so much in my bloody life.

She presses her drink bottle to her lips and tilts her head back, gulping the water and quenching her thirst. A little bit of the water misses her mouth and travels down her chin to trickle slowly between her breasts.

Now, I want nothing more than to be that droplet of water. *Fuck! I need her.*

Stalking her like she is prey I'm about to devour, I walk along the windows to my office, not taking my eyes from her mouthwatering form. My dick seems to have a mind of its own, escalating its request to explore her depths. And believe me, I'm more than inclined to grant this ardent appeal.

She turns, bends over and places her water and towel on the ground. I can't help but pause in my pacing of the window to stare at her arse which is primed and positioned for me to grab hold of ... I'm completely done for. Cock-stunned and fuck-ready.

'That's it!' I groan.

Eagerly striding toward the door which leads into the apartment, I'm halted by the ring of my phone.

'What now?' I growl at the plastic telecommunications device from hell, the bane of my existence.

Walking back to my desk, I hit the speaker button and bark like a vicious animal. 'What?'

'Bryce, sorry, have I caught you at a bad time. Is everything all right?' Arthur asks, concern manifesting in his voice.

How this man manages to find the most inappropriate times to interrupt amazes me.

'Yes, Arthur, everything is fine. But I am in the middle of something,' I say through gritted teeth, as I watch Alexis now performing knee raises on the power tower.

Her gaze travels to my window and she struggles to smile as she strains and lifts her legs.

I smile back.

'I'm sorry, but this can't wait. There has been an incident downstairs on the casino floor.'

Eyes still trained on Alexis, I watch as she blows me a kiss. *Fuck!*

I drop my head back and close my eyes in heated frustration. 'What kind of incident?'

'Armed hold-up at one of the cashier booths, sir.'

Breathing in deeply, I turn around and take a seat at my desk. 'Which one?' I ask, as I access the casino's security feed through my laptop.

'Booth six. Dale has the assailant in the holding cell, and the police are on their way.'

I find the security files for Cashier Booth Six. 'How long ago did this happen?'

'Approximately five to seven minutes.'

I click on the file date-stamped eight minutes ago and begin to watch the feed. Before long, I notice an agitated Caucasian male pointing a handgun at Selena, one of my long-term employees. Selena is a fifty-four-year-old mother of three and has been working for me for over twelve years.

'Shit! Is Selena okay?' I ask, running my hands through my hair.

'She's a little shaken, but she's fine.'

'How the hell did this creep go unnoticed?' I question, furious that our state-of-the-art facial recognition software and highly trained security officers were unable to prevent this attack.

'I don't have the details yet, but obviously we will have to review the entire event. Dale is waiting for you in the cell, but if you are busy —'

'No, I'll be there. Just give me minute.'

'Okay. See you soon.'

I hang up from Arthur and drop my head in my hands.

'Is everything all right?' Alexis asks as she makes her way toward my desk with Brayden against her chest.

The sight of both them rips my aggravation away like tearing off a Band-Aid.

'Yes, everything is fine. But I have to head downstairs for a moment. There was an armed hold-up on the casino floor.'

'Shit! Is everyone okay? God! Nobody got hurt, did they?'

Putting my arms out, I indicate I want to cuddle my son and Alexis obligingly hands Brayden over to me. The mixture of his pure, baby smell and the soft scent of Alexis' perfume has me feeling at peace once again.

I sigh a little and answer to put her at ease. 'Selena, the cashier who bore the brunt of his threat, is apparently a little shaken. I want to go and see if she is all right and gather a few more details as to how this happened.'

'Of course, I'll cancel my afternoon with —'

'No, don't do that. You deserve an afternoon of pampering with your friends. It's long overdue.'

'It's okay. It's only hair, massage and some waxing. It really isn't that important.'

'Honey,' I say, as I touch the side of her face, 'you're going. I promise this won't take long. And anyway, I'm looking forward to a bit of just-me-and-the-kids time.'

The buzzer to the door sounds, interrupting us.

A huge smile covers her face. 'You are, are you?'

Instantly, I sense her smile and tone of voice holds hidden meaning. 'What's that supposed to mean?'

She takes Brayden from me and, like always, the feeling of loss is unpleasant.

'Nothing,' she replies, clearly full of shit.

I would've interrogated her further, but she opens the door to my office and is nearly thrown back by a massive bunch of blue and white balloons.

Lil — the bearer of those balloons — awkwardly stumbles through the door. 'Hello, congratulations! Let me see, let me see,' she squawks, while letting go of the helium filled bunch she is holding. The balloons hit the roof and bob around.

Following Lil through the door is Carly and Jade, then Steph holding a big green dinosaur and a bunch of flowers. They all gather around Alexis and Brayden and coo at my little man like he is the most adorable sight to be seen. Well ... I can't really blame them. He is.

Smiling, I shake my head and get ready to head out the door.

'Where's Tash?' Alexis asks, disappointment appearing across her face. 'Don't tell me she can't make it.'

The girls laugh, except for Lil who just rolls her eyes and places her hands on her hips. 'She refused to ride in the elevator with the balloons,' Lil deadpans.

Alexis looks to the roof and cracks up laughing. 'Oh yeah ... I forgot she has a phobia of balloons. Funniest thing ever.'

A phobia is far from the 'funniest thing ever' ... I should know. But balloons? Yeah, that is pretty amusing.

Just as I'm about to kiss Alexis and Brayden goodbye, Tash enters the room and gives the spot where the balloons have rested against the roof a very wide birth while eyeing them suspiciously. 'Keep those fuckers away from me. I swear, Lil, if you pull the shit you just pulled downstairs with those evil things again, I will cut you. I'm not kidding.'

'That's my cue to leave,' I announce. 'I'll be back soon.'

I kiss Alexis and Brayden goodbye and then head out of the room. As I'm walking to the elevator, I hear Alexis ask what shit Lil pulled.

'She locked Tash in the car with them,' Steph explains. 'It was hilarious.'

'Yeah, ha ha ... very funny,' Tash responds. 'I'm scarred for freakin' life.'

I smile and shake my head, but soon frown at the thought of being locked in the car with a clown. That shit is just not funny.

***

After spending a little time with Selena and praising her for staying calm and following protocol, I reaffirm she was safe by reminding her that the cashier booths are bulletproof. I send Selena home on extended leave and organise some counselling for her. Despite the fact it is company policy anyway, I want her to feel well looked after.

I'm then briefed by Dale — my head of security — that the assailant is a desperate drug user and not the sharpest tool in the shed. I make it very clear that I want a full rundown of the circumstances; exactly how did a shady character — looking the way the dickhead looks — get into the casino in the first place. I then leave Dale to handle the police and manage the aftermath.

Opening the door to my apartment, I find Alexis breastfeeding Brayden while sitting around the lounge with her friends.

'I swear, I shot milk a good metre away,' Steph says proudly.

'Yeah, well, I could write Jade on the shower screen,' Jade explains as she grabs at her breasts and mimics the lettering of J.a.d.e.

What. The. Fuck?

'Yuck! You two are disgusting. I'm not having kids for that reason alone. No one should be able to write their name with liquid from their boobs,' Carly interjects.

I tend to agree with her.

'Oh, grow up,' Lil grumbles. 'When you have that much milk in your ducts, you can't help it. It just squirts out.'

Feeling the need to end this conversation before I hear something I will never be able to wipe from my memory bank, I make it known that I am standing in the room. 'Ladies, sorry I took so long.'

I head over to Alexis, kiss her forehead, then cup Brayden's head in my hand and rub his earlobe with my thumb. Hearing what sounds like a loving sigh, I look up to find Steph staring at me, all dreamy like a bloody teenager. I give her an awkward smile just as Jade elbows her in the ribs.

'Here you go, Daddy,' Alexis says, handing me my very milk-groggy son. 'He needs to burp and he also needs his nappy changed. I should only be gone for three hours. Ring me if you need anything and I'll come straight up. If he happens to get hungry again, or I'm running a little late, there's backup milk that I've expressed in a bottle in the fridge. He's got a little nappy rash, so don't forget the cream and —'

'Go!' I demand, kissing her worried face and stopping her rant. 'We'll be fine. Won't we, Bray?' I ask, giving him a fist bump. 'Go and enjoy yourselves.'

'Bye kids,' Alexis calls out, Nate and Charli reciprocating their acknowledgement by shouting back.

Carly links her arm around Alexis' and practically drags her to the front door, Tash giving her arse little smacks on the way there. I'm momentarily jealous, wanting to be the one giving her arse small smacks, not only with my hand, but with my hips and ...

Brayden's little cry snaps me out of my light bondage fantasy of Alexis. 'Shit! Burp, that's right,' I murmur to myself. 'Sorry, buddy.'

I drape the burping cloth over my shoulder and hoist him up gently, patting his back as I walk upstairs toward his nursery. Seconds later, he lets out a noise that I'm fairly sure was not solely a burp.

'That did not sound good, Bray,' I state, a little concerned. 'That sounded wet.'

Passing Charli's bedroom, I find her lying on her stomach on the floor, colouring in. 'Hey, Charlotte. What you doin'?'

'Drawing Addison a best friend picture. Do you like it?' she asks, holding up a pink piece of paper covered in girly pictures and sparkly shit.

'Yeah, it's ... girly.'

Charlotte giggles. 'Of course it's girly, silly. Addison is a girl. I can't give her a boy picture.'

As per usual, the little lady is correct.

'No, you can't,' I say with a smile as I turn and head toward Brayden's nursery.

'Um ... Bryce?'

'Yeah,' I call back, twisting around.

Charlotte screws up her face and points toward me. 'You have baby spew on your back.'

I twist further and catch a glimpse of a white trail down my shirt. 'Gee, thanks, Brayden. Just what Daddy has always wanted. Come on, looks like we are both getting changed.'

'Can I help?' Charlotte calls out.

'Sure.'

We enter the nursery, and I automatically smile at the space theme Alexis and I agreed on. Stepping in here reminds me a little of being in the observatory. Painted on the walls and roof are constellations, planets and spaceships. Okay, so the spaceships don't remind me of the observatory, but the rest does.

Right before I lay Brayden down on the change table, he lets one rip, except like the burp beforehand, it sounds incredibly wet.

'Please don't tell me you did what I think you just did?' I groan.

He grunts a little, reinforcing that, yes ... he did.

'Er, what's that smell?' Charli whines, pinching her nostrils.

'What do you think it is?' I ask, not really requiring an answer.

'Brayden, did you just do poo-poo in your nappy?' Still pinching her nostrils, Charlotte drops her head close to his face. 'Poo-poo is for the potty.'

He widens his eyes at her closeness, seeming to adjust his tiny vision.

'He's a bit young for the potty, Charlotte.'

'Starlight's a baby and she uses the potty.'

Who the fuck is Starlight?

I look at her a little perplexed. 'Who's Starlight?'

'My baby doll.'

'Oh.' I don't really know what to say to that.

Unbuttoning his little blue onesie, I soon become horrifyingly aware that yes, the wind he not long ago broke was not wind at all. Instead, what is filling his nappy and spilling out over the sides, is my worst nightmare.

'Aw, Brayden ... what the crap, buddy.'

I lift his legs out of his onesie only to find the mushy shit has found its way down them as well. *Ah, shit! It just keeps getting worse.*

Charlotte spots the poo-splosion and takes a step back. 'That's just gross.'

'Tell me about it,' I agree wholeheartedly.

As I attempt to free his arms as well, his little hands clench the sleeves, preventing my efforts. *Why are these stupid onesies called Wondersuits? There's nothing fucking wonderful about them.*

'Brayden, let go,' I laugh at him with frustration, as I gently try to pry his fingers apart.

He does as he's told — well, technically not — and I get him free from his suit. Except now I have to tackle the singlet ... which I'm pretty fucking sure was white when Alexis put it on him this morning. Now looking at it, it's a yellowish brown and stuck to his skin. *Why do babies have to wear so much bloody clothing?*

'Shit!' I curse to myself, now beginning to stress out.

'Don't swear,' Charlotte says from behind.

I twist around to find her inconspicuously taking steps backward toward the door. 'Where are you going?' *Don't you bloody abandon me now.*

'To my room.'

'You said you wanted to help.'

'That was before I saw that,' she says, pointing to Brayden's nappy.

'You can't leave. I need all hands on deck ... Nate!' I shout, hoping for an extra set of them.

Within seconds, Nate comes into the room looking worried. 'What?'

'I have a situation with your brother,' I explain as calmly as possible.

'Don't do it, Nate,' Charlotte warns. 'Don't go any closer.'

'What's wrong? What's that sme—'

'That smell is what Brayden is covered in and no doubt soon to be covering me.'

I hate to admit it, but I cannot see any way out of becoming victim to his mess.

'Right. And what do you want me to do about it?' Nate asks, now stepping back to where Charlotte is standing.

'Pass me things.'

'What things?'

Good fucking question.

'Um ... wipes. I need wipes! But first get one of those smelly bag thingies.'

'I'll get the bag,' Charlotte pipes up.

Nate moves to my side. 'I'm on the wipes.'

'Good. Let's get this *shit* sorted.'

'Don't swear,' Charli says again.

'Sorry,' I mutter, feeling a little less overwhelmed.

Cringing like a Goddamn pansy, I peel Brayden's singlet from his tiny chest, lifting it over his head and accidentally wiping some of the shit on his cheek. *Fuck! Sorry, little mate.*

'Ew, you just wiped poo on his face,' Charlotte complains.

'Sh, I didn't mean it. Don't tell your mum,' I plead like an idiot. 'Hold the bag out.'

She holds the bag out and I drop the singlet in it.

'Wipe!' I command, now sounding somewhat like an army sergeant. 'On second thoughts, Nate, make that a few wipes.'

He hands me a whole bunch of them, and I wipe the shit off Brayden's cheek then tackle his back and tummy. Soon, we seem to have the situation under control, the mushy poo-smeared nappy and clothing in a bag.

Looking down at Brayden's Mr Doodle — *bloody hell! Alexis and her stupid nicknames* — I fret for the smallest of seconds after discovering I don't have it covered and the last thing I need after cleaning him up is having piss everywhere.

Quickly, I grab a nappy and place it over the top of his unpredictable little fella, and then sigh with relief. 'Okay, Nate, grab another singlet and suit, please,' I say, and wait for the fresh items of clothing.

'What do I do with this?' Charlotte asks, standing like a statue and still holding the bag with the poo-covered clothes and nappy in it.

'Rubbish bin.'

'Mum won't be happy if you throw his clothes away.'

'Don't be silly. We can't keep those. They are covered in shit.'

'Don't swear.'

'Where has this "don't swear" shit come from?'

'Don't swear. And Nanny told me to say it. She said you and Mummy swear a lot.'

I chuckle to myself. *Bloody Maryann.*

Nate hands me the clean clothing and another wipe even though I don't need one. 'She's right, Mum won't be happy if she finds out you threw away Brayden's clothes.'

'Thanks, mate. But I don't need any more wipes.'

'Yes, you do. You have poo on your head and arm.'

Looking at my arm and now becoming acutely aware of a smear on my head, I shudder and wipe both spots. 'Thanks. Okay, baby boy, let's get you dressed.'

I place a clean nappy under his bottom and go to secure it.

'You need to put some of that white cream on his bottom,' Charli reminds me.

'Yes, yes, I do.'

Thankful for my little helpers, I take the nappy rash cream Charlotte is holding out for me and wipe a bit on Brayden's bum. I am now happy and content that I have covered all bases where this nappy change debacle is concerned, so I reclothe Brayden and pick him up, holding him in the air just like Simba in the *Lion King*.

He smiles at me.

Hold the fuck on ... he just smiled at me.

'He's smiling,' Nate says with a laugh, while pointing to his baby brother.

Leaning in closer for a better look, I smile back. 'He is, isn't he?'

Despite the past hour and the nightmare he was the cause of, his smile fills my heart with happiness. He is my pride and joy.

CHAPTER TWELVE

'Do it again,' I probe, pulling ridiculous faces at Brayden. 'Come on, smile for Daddy.'

'It was just wind, Bryce,' Alexis deadpans from the sofa.

Lying on my side on the floor next to Brayden, I desperately try to get him to smile like he had before. 'No, it wasn't, he smiled. Nate, tell your Mum he smiled.'

'Yeah, Mum, he did. Right after he did the biggest poo in history. It was disgusting.'

Alexis laughs and looks at me sympathetically. Her hair is now shorter, much shorter, sitting just below her shoulders. She looks incredibly cute in a sexy way.

'He will only be four weeks old tomorrow. I think it's too early for him to smile,' she says with sympathy, while flipping the page of her magazine.

'He smiled,' I repeat, not having it any other way.

Alexis puts down her magazine and looks toward the kids. 'So what's for dinner, ratbags?'

'McDonalds,' they both chant.

Shit! I hate McDonalds.

I look up at Alexis and shoot her a you'll-pay-for-this look. She innocently bites her bottom lip and smiles. There's no way I can fight that smile and she knows it. It's her ultimate weapon. That, and the one between her legs.

Compassionately patting me on the thigh like I'm some elderly frail man, she offers me an out. 'It's okay, I'll go get it.'

God! I'm pathetic. 'No. I'll get it,' I say, shaking my head and rolling my eyes at her as if to say that I'm quite capable of going to the horrid place and that it doesn't faze me in the slightest. When, truth be told, it does; it fucking fazes me immensely. I hate with a vengeance having to go anywhere near Ronald McFucking Donald with his bright red scary hair, yellow fucktard suit, pasty white powdery skin and obscenely high eyebrows. How the hell he doesn't bother every person on this planet mystifies me.

'Charli-Bear,' Alexis says, clasping Charlotte's hand in hers while making it extremely obvious that she is trying to keep a straight face, 'I think you should go with Bryce.' She raises an eyebrow at Charlotte, hinting I need someone to hold my hand.

I know what she's doing and she thinks she is funny. She also thinks she is going to get away with it, but she's not. No. Way. In. Hell.

Charlotte looks over at me and nods her head as though I'm her new-found charity case. My balls basically evaporate.

'Come on then, Charlotte,' I say as I get up off the ground.

Charli walks over to the door and waits while Alexis swaps places with me. As Alexis bends down on her knees, I lean in to kiss her neck and gently whisper in her ear. 'I like your hair. I like it so much that I'm going to grab a fistful of it tonight while I fuck you into the next century.'

I walk toward the door and briefly look back, finding Alexis still on her hands and knees watching me with hungry eyes and a salacious grin. Her arse is perfectly poised in the air, and if it weren't for the three children in the room, I wouldn't hesitate to yank down her jeans, rip her underwear to shreds, and plant my cock so fucking deep inside her pussy, I'd be more than balls deep.

Lingering probably just a little too long on her rear end, I click my neck to the side and clench my fists, taking a second to get my shit back together before focussing on my trip to McFucking Hell.

***

'Why are you scared of clowns?' Charlotte asks as we walk through the entertainment precinct.

'Mr Clark,' one of my security team acknowledges as we pass by.

I nod back at him, then answer Charli. 'Because they are weird-looking.'

'Are you scared of ET?'

'No. Why?' I ask, a little perplexed by her randomness.

'Because he's weird-looking, too.'

Huh, she has a point.

'Are you scared of sloths?'

I have to think for a second about what a sloth actually looks like. 'No, I don't think so.'

'They are REALLY weird-looking.'

'I'll take your word for it, Charli.'

We turn the corner, and once again I'm greeted with the evil statue sitting on the park bench-style seat like he owns the fucking joint. *Newsflash, McFuckhead, I own it.*

I purposely keep my distance as I approach the counter. Charli, however, decides to take a seat next to him.

It makes me cringe with disgust.

'Bryce, come sit with me,' she proposes, smiling sweetly at me.

'Nope, I'm good. What do you want, Charlotte? A Happy Meal?' I ask, wanting to get this McShit ordered so I can get the McHell out of here.

All of a sudden Charlotte bursts into pretend tears. And I mean *really* bursts into pretend tears, howling loudly like she is auditioning for the cowardly lion in *The Wizard of Oz*.

I look around slightly dumbfounded, noticing others looking her way as well.

'Charlotte, what are you doing?' I whisper under my breath. Her howl gains a few decibels.

Feeling uncomfortable as it is — by having to be here in the first place — I am now in the equivalent of hell, taking in the bystanders giving me dirty looks. I realise it's because I'm just standing here while an innocent little girl is crying.

Bloody hell!

'Charlotte, come here. Tell me what's wrong.'

'No,' she faux sobs while peeking through her finger-covered face. 'You come here.'

You cheeky little shit! You are just like your mother. I'm both furious and impressed with her efforts to get me closer to the statue of Satan.

An elderly lady touches me on the arm. 'Is she all right?'

'She's fine,' I reassure the nosey woman then begrudgingly make my way over to Charlotte. I kneel in front of her and ignore the statue with every fibre of my being. 'You're making a scene, Charli —'

She drops her hands from her face with lightning speed and clasps mine which I've placed on her knees. Her eyes are wide like saucers, wide and dry ... completely tear-free.

'He's not real,' she whispers, focussing intently on my face.

I feel her lift my hand and move it toward the statue. *What. The. Fuck?*

I go to pull my hand away, but she secures it with her other hand, now having both hands wrapped around mine. Intrigued by the determination in her face — because let's face it, I could lift her up and out of this seat with my pinky finger — I play along for a second.

'I'm not touching the statue,' I say with stern words.

'Yes, you are. You need to,' she retorts, just as sternly.

'Charlotte. I. Am. Not. Touching. That. Statue,' I say again through gritted teeth, placing her hand back on her knee.

She doesn't let go of mine, and this time her faux sadness becomes real. 'I don't want you to be scared.'

In this moment, my heart fills with love. 'Sweetheart, I don't want to be either. But I can't help it.'

'But Bryce, look at him. He is just paint and,' she knocks on his leg, 'plastic?'

I drop my head, knowing she's right. Apart from the plastic — technically, he's fibreglass.

Breathing in deeply and drawing on every bit of willpower I own, I look up and place my hand on Ronald's knee. 'Is that better?'

'I don't know, you tell me,' she says with a tear-filled smile.

So much like her mother.

I stand, pulling her up with me and placing her on my hip. Then I lie. 'Yeah, much better.'

***

Later that night after the kids are in bed and Brayden is asleep for what we hope is at least six hours, I walk into the en suite to the sound of the shower running and Alexis humming what I soon make out is Cold Chisel's 'Flame Trees'.

Propping myself against the doorframe, I watch as she soaps her body. She has her back to me, which I'm thankful for, because it affords me a little extra time to take in the curved silky body that rocks my world.

Grabbing my t-shirt from behind, I pull it over my head and drop it to the floor quietly, so that I don't alert her to my presence. I want to surprise her.

Unbuttoning my jeans, I pull them down over my already hard dick and, taking myself in my hand, I slowly palm my length to ease the intense throbbing that has surfaced.

I'm eager to touch every inch of her, so I make way into the shower and secure her from behind, cupping her pussy with one hand and placing the other on her neck. She jolts in surprise for the split second it takes her to realise I am the one holding her captive.

'It's been twenty-seven days since I've been inside you, Alexis. Twenty-seven fucking agonising days,' I whisper harshly in her ear.

My finger flexes and massages the soft skin of her clit, while my other hand firmly clenches her neck, but not enough to make her feel uncomfortable.

She moans and her legs weaken, but being so attuned to her body, I predict this movement and support her waning frame.

'Can you feel my cock on your arse?' I question, nipping at her ear before running my tongue along the back of her neck. 'How hard I am?'

An indistinct word is mumbled from her mouth as I press my finger deeper into her wet skin. Alexis begins to rock her hips against my hand, and her head falls back onto my shoulder, baring her neck. I loosen my grip and lightly trail my hand up and down her neckline.

'Please tell me I can fuck you.'

With her eyes still closed and water streaming down her chest, she licks her lips. 'You can.'

I let out a growl, something I do often when around this woman. 'That's not what I asked you to say.'

I want her to tell me I can fuck her; I want to hear those dirty little words, beg for it.

Alexis tilts her head to face me, grabs a handful of my hair and brings my mouth to hers, all the while forcing my finger inside her pussy. 'You can fuck me,' she mutters aggressively.

My body responds to her request, tensing, magnetising to her soft, wet skin. I slide my finger in and out of her and augment it with a second, gently stretching her in preparation for my cock.

The last thing I want to do is hurt her; after all, it's only been four weeks since she gave birth.

'Does that feel good?' I ask her, making sure she is enjoying what I'm doing.

Her body indicates that she does, but I want to hear her say it ... purr it.

'Yes, it feels ... so good,' she moans.

I press my mouth to hers again and stroke her tongue with my own, tasting all she has to offer. She is my delicacy; my desired flavour.

Alexis breaks away from my mouth and bends forward, placing her palms flat against the tiled wall and widening her stance. Dropping my hand from her throat, I glide it down in between her breasts, only to rest it upon her hip.

With a delectable moan slowly pouring out of her mouth, she presses her arse against the crown of my dick, allowing me to glide and swirl it around her opening.

'Fuck,' I grind out, now desperate to feel her pussy walls clenching around my cock.

Slowly, I press into her, closing my eyes in tune with the superb sensation of her warmth. It has been twenty-seven days of waiting. The air surrounding her mouth is sharply inhaled, and it worries me for a split second that she isn't quite ready even though she says she is.

Just as I am about to withdraw, she lets out the most erotic-sounding moan with enough ardour to rival the steam in the shower.

'Oh god, Bryce. I've missed you, I've missed this.'

'I've missed you too, honey, more than you'll ever know.'

Encouraged by her gratification and obvious euphoria, I proceed to hold her hips and drive into her with timed precision, my glide effortless — she's so wet and primed for me.

When I'm feeling this fucking ravenous and alive with pent-up sexual tension, I need to remind myself to be careful, and not get carried away for fear of hurting her. So I pull out and spin her around to face me, which always brings me back to a safer momentum.

Lifting her back onto my cock, I impale her and press her against the wall, my sudden change of position forcing her to gasp. With her lips now parted, I ravage her mouth, seeking out her tongue with my own as I continue to drive into her, relishing the feel of her body once again joined with mine. I realise just how much I have missed being inside her, holding her, hearing the raw, carnal noises reverberate from within. I've simply missed making love to the woman I love.

Okay, I realise this can be seen as ridiculous. In hindsight, it has been less than a month since I last had sex with her. The thing is, the power of addiction is a force to be reckoned with; a dependence that can only be cured with determination. And where Alexis is concerned, my resolve is non-existent.

Feeling the build-up of pressure at the head of my dick, I explode into her like Mount Fucking Vesuvius and growl like a goddamn barbarian, my release too long in waiting.

***

Following our lovemaking from the night before, you'd think I'd be one happy, relaxed and fully sated man. But I'm not, not completely anyway. Yes, my balls now feel a little more like the billiard variety and a lot less like the bowling variety, I can't dispute that. The thing is, today I'm anxious for an entirely different reason; today is Gareth's birthday and I can't seem to get him out of my mind, or off my conscience.

Sitting here at my desk, I replay the final conversation I had with him on the morning his psychotic alter, Scott, held Alexis hostage and nearly killed her. I'd been so wrapped up and absorbed in my own life, I had not paid attention to Gareth's state of mind and body language, completely failing to see just how out of control his condition really was. I'd fooled myself into believing that he was taking his meds because I'd asked him to do so, never having thought to check that the pills he was actually taking were, in fact, the prescribed ones. Apparently, he had been popping vitamins in my presence.

Now, nine months down the track, I can clearly see — as I look back on those weeks leading up to the explosion — that his behaviour and conduct were not only irrational, but evidently disturbed. Things like the angry phone call I received after Christmas, when he accused Alexis of deliberately omitting him from our family lunch. Not to mention the numerous phone calls and emails I got while Alexis and I were in Italy — emails checking on Clark Incorporated issues that did not concern him. All these things I'd just swept under the rug, because for once in my life — ever since the car accident occurred — I didn't want to have to deal with Gareth, didn't want to be responsible for babysitting him. Except the moment I did drop my guard and responsibility, the worst possible thing happened ... I failed him.

Sitting on the edge of our bed, I watch Alexis peacefully enjoying her slumber. She has no choice but to sleep on her back, because apparently if she sleeps on her stomach she'll wake up in a puddle of breast milk. As I stare at her glorious breasts, which are hidden behind her maternity bra — a crime in itself — I yearn to caress the soft flesh with my tongue.

The imposed nipple prohibition is slowly killing me, eating at my sanity and diminishing my tenacity. Having no choice but to fight my nipple-need, I think of a distraction.

A smile creeps onto my face as an idea of something I know she loves, but something I haven't done in a while, takes form. I race downstairs and grab a yellow rose from the vase in the foyer then race back upstairs and kneel on the ground next to the bed. I am excited just like a kid on Christmas Day, all because I love waking her up with a rose.

Very lightly, I wipe the bud of the flower across her forehead, this prompting her brow to crease ever so slightly. Her rose-taunted face is adorable and I have to bite my lip to suppress a laugh.

Returning the rose to the bridge of her nose, I trail it downward very softly. Her hand swings up out of nowhere and swipes at what her subconscious is telling her is there. I quickly retract the rose before she touches it and, with a mischievous inward chuckle, wait patiently for her to settle again. She does, and as I take in her serene appearance, I melt with love. Her eyelashes are long and black, and fan beautifully atop her cheekbones. She has some very faint freckles, and the last time I counted there were about nineteen of them across her nose and cheeks. Her lips are downright irresistible, plump and semi-pursed. And her blonde hair neatly frames the most beautiful face in the world.

Swallowing the lump in my throat and smiling because I know how fortunate I am, I place the rose on her lips and sit it just under her nose, knowing that when she inhales her next breath, the scent she loves so much will filter into her senses and will begin to wake her from sleep. I watch with fascination as she breathes in a deep breath, her chest rising as her hands find her hair while she stretches. Her eyelids flutter open and within seconds she begins to decipher what is before her. When she does interpret what her eyes are seeing, her heartbreaking smile starts to spread across her face. And, as always when she graces me with that expression, I am conquered ... done for.

'Mornin',' she mumbles, and sits up on her elbows while taking the rose from my hand.

'Mornin',' I reply, leaning down to kiss those perfect lips.

She drops back onto the pillow and wraps her arms around my neck, securing me tightly to her. 'You're dressed. Why are you dressed? You should be butt-naked and underneath me.'

Wanting to be butt-naked and underneath her, I contemplate that actual scenario before reminding myself why I am dressed and ready to leave. 'I have an appointment. I'll be gone for an hour.'

'Okay,' she pouts.

'Don't do that.'

Her pout increases. 'What?'

'You know what.' I lean forward and suck on her pouty lip. 'I've to go,' I say sadly.

She unwraps her arms and places both hands on either side of my face. 'Is everything all right?'

Feeling her enquiring stare pierce deep into the depths of my eyes, I lie. 'Yeah, I'm fine. Just want to get this done so that I can get back here to my favourite people in the world.'

She nods and kisses me lightly, then lets me go and, just as I stand, movement from Brayden's bassinet catches my attention. I creep over slowly — probably looking somewhat like a fucking cat burglar — and find my little treasure trying desperately to free his hand from his tightly confining wrap. Smiling, I notice the little Houdini has already managed to release one of his hands and is sucking on it ferociously.

'Good morning, little buddy. I'm sorry to tell to you, but it doesn't matter how hard you suck on that hand, you're not going to get what you want out of it.' He lets out a frustrated cry. 'I know. Life's not fair. I want Mummy's boobies in my mouth all the time too.'

A sharp sting to the arm registers as I incur Alexis' swift slap. 'Bryce!'

I lift Brayden up, giving him a quick cuddle and kiss before handing him to his mum. 'Right,' I say with annoyance, wanting to stay with them, 'I'll be back soon.'

Making my way out of the room, I prepare myself for my visit to Gareth's grave.

CHAPTER THIRTEEN

To feel contrite is a humane and moral virtue, but in order to experience this form of repentance, you must first acknowledge your sin then show remorse for your wrongdoing. Jessica has made it quite clear that she does not agree with my sense of contrition where Gareth's death is concerned, saying I have no sin to feel remorseful over in the first place, but she is wrong.

For the past nine months, Jessica and I have had session upon session where she has tried desperately to conquer my inner battle with guilt using her own personal army of professional advocacy. The thing is, not all battles are fought and then won.

A perfect battle would end in a resolution always being achieved, whether by annihilating the opposition, or forcing them to abandon their mission and surrender their forces. And that's exactly what Jessica's warfare strategy, where my battle is concerned, has been of late: the implementation of tactics to break my resolve and renounce my fight with myself. And I have to admit, it's starting to work.

I hadn't wanted to, but I humoured her and put myself in Lucy's shoes, looking at the entire situation from another perspective. Did it make me feel less guilty? No. Did I still feel contrite? Yes, I did, because at the end of the day, I could have prevented Gareth's death. However, the reason for me deciding to wave the white flag after so long was Jessica's argument during our last session about not letting the guilt 'eat me alive'. It helped me realise that for Brayden and Alexis' sake, I needed to ask for my own forgiveness. Jessica had said that if I couldn't find it within myself to see that I was not at fault in the first place, then I had to apologise and make amends for what blame I felt I had. And the first step in doing that was to visit Gareth's grave and say sorry.

Hearing my phone ring through the Bluetooth of my Lamborghini, I take note of Lucy's name on the screen. 'How's my favourite sister?' I say as I take the call, going for the buttering-up type of approach.

'Your *only* sister is fine. It's her brother she is worried about, today of all days.'

Shit! Why was she born with an IQ to rival Einstein?

'Don't know what you're talking 'bout, baby sis. I'm fine.'

'Don't pull that shit with me. We made each other a promise a long time ago, remember? Telling each other everything goes both ways, not just when it suits you.'

Inwardly groaning to myself, I click my neck to both sides then fess up. 'I'm on my way to the cemetery, Luce. I need to get a few things off my chest ...' I pause for the slightest second then continue. 'It was Jessica's idea, and for once, I'm listening to it,' I finish, with not much enthusiasm in my voice.

'Do you want me to meet you there?'

'No, really, I'm fine. I just need to get this done so that I can move on and live my life. A life I have waited so long to live unburdened.'

Lucy sighs. 'Okay, but if you need me, you know I'm here.'

'I know,' I sigh back.

I'm about to say my goodbyes when her choked voice sounds quietly through my speakers. 'I love you. I respect you. I look up to you and only want the best for you.'

Feeling that horrid thump in my chest when I know I have to rein my shit in before I cry like a kid, I take a deep breath and focus on the traffic ahead. 'I love you too, Luce. Always.'

***

The light spring breeze whispers across my face as I walk the gravel path I have walked many times before. It's a sombre walk, full of sadness, and no matter how many times or for how long I have done it, it still leaves me feeling partly empty.

With a bunch of lilies in my hand, I stop by Mum, Dad and Lauchie's graves first. This is the first time I have been here since becoming a father and, for some reason unknown to me, I am bearing extra emotion.

I lay the lilies down for my mother and whisper to her headstone, never really understanding why I do it. Deep down, I know I'm talking to a slab of granite.

'Mum, guess what? I have a son and he's ... he's perfect. His name is Brayden ... Brayden Lauchie Clark.'

I look over to my little brother's resting place, 'Did you hear that Lauch? Yeah, he shares your name.'

Taking a small photograph of Brayden out of my pocket, I place it at the base of Mum's headstone. 'You can have this for now. But I promise I'll bring him by soon.'

I don't want to linger too long, because I hate coming here on my own. I stand up and take a step closer to Dad's place of rest. Touching the top of his headstone, I say four words that now hold so much meaning: 'I get it now.'

As I'm about to move on to Gareth's grave, I hear footsteps on the gravel path behind me. They could belong to only one of two people, and as I feel her hand slide into mine, I have no doubt who she is — warmth and a sense of fulfilment now flowing freely though me.

'You should've told me,' Alexis whispers into my ear as she rests her head on my shoulder.

I squeeze her hand, knowing that I should've confided in her.

'It's okay, though,' she continues. 'I understand you need to do certain things on your own. But I want you to know, you are never alone. I'll wait for you over there until you're finished, okay?'

I nod and she releases my hand before kissing me softly. She then bends down and places a new book on Lauchie's grave. I notice its title: *Tomorrow, When the War Began* and smile. Unbeknown to her, it was one of his favourites.

While Alexis stands patiently by an elm tree, I say the few words to Gareth I'd planned on saying. 'I let you down, mate, and for that, I'm sorry. I'm sorry that you were the one in the car with Mum, Dad and Lauchie all those years ago. I'm sorry that you were the one to hold Lauchie in your arms while his life slipped away from him. I'm sorry that you never got to live the life you deserved. And I'm sorry you died because of me.'

Sucking in a deep breath, I will the tears not to fall. I refuse to let them fall, I don't deserve to cry. 'Gareth, I'm sorry, but I'm a father now, and my son deserves a dad who knows how to accept responsibility for his own actions, yet also forgive himself and move on with his life. I hope you can forgive me too.'

I wait for a minute and turn around to see Alexis push off from the tree and start walking toward me. She's wearing a long flowing pale pink dress with a cream scarf tied around her neck. Her hair is twisted back and held together with a clip. As she closes the gap between us, a gust of wind sweeps her dress and scarf to the side, taking what breath I have along with it. She is just beyond beautiful.

'Are you ready?' she asks, taking both my hands and holding them in front of us.

I think about the simple question she just asked but interpret it in a different way. *Yes, I am ready.*

I'm ready to live the rest of my life with the woman I love.

PART TWO

Thief of my heart

CHAPTER FOURTEEN

Since becoming a father I have felt many wonderful things: awe, pride, satisfaction; the ability to take on the entire world and those who are in it. Unfortunately, the wonderful joys of fatherhood seem to go hand in hand with the not so wonderful joys, such as confusion, panic and complete exhaustion. All at the hands of one tiny little human being.

Today, my baby boy turns one. Yes, one! As in 365 days old, those days being the best in my life. It feels as if it were only yesterday that I heard his cry, touched his face, looked into his eyes and held him, all for the first time. I just can't believe how quickly this past year has flown by.

Since that miraculous day, I have experienced so much more of what life has to offer. I've experienced hearing the words 'Dad Dad' spoken in such rapid succession that no matter how many times Brayden said it, it still took me several seconds to register that he was, in fact, referring to me as his dad for the first time. I've experienced severe sleep deprivation, sex deprivation and a scarcity of pure silence. I also now know what it feels like to freak the fuck out, and I mean *really* freak out.

When Brayden was ten months old, he somehow managed to get a pea stuck up his nose while he was eating his dinner. And do you think for the life of me that I was able to get it out ... not a chance in hell.

I remember trying to dislodge it with my fingernail, which was inevitably a failure due to his nostril being too bloody small and my finger resembling one that belonged to a giant. So there I was, completely stressed out, panicked and with my phone in my hand about to dial triple 0, when in walked Alexis, calm and composed.

'What's wrong?' she'd asked, obviously sensing from the petrified look on my face that something was clearly out of the ordinary.

Not wanting to waste any more precious time, I explained. 'Bray has a pea stuck up his nose. I'm calling an ambulance.'

She rolled her eyes, took one look at Brayden and, I shit you not, smiled at him. I had started to voice my concern that perhaps it was not the time for smiling, when she gently blocked his other nostril and blew in his mouth, sending the pea flying out onto the benchtop. Alexis then scooped it up, placed it in my hand and picked up Brayden, walking off with him jiggling on her hip and saying, 'silly dadda.' Let's just say I stood there for god knows how long, looking incredulously at the pea that was now in my hand.

Another freak out moment was only the other day when I was cooking dinner. Brayden was playing by my feet banging on the pots and pans I had given him, together with a wooden spoon. One minute he was there and the next he wasn't. I swear the kid has a hidden turbo button which allows him to crawl at high speed when you turn your head for the smallest of seconds. Needless to say, I found him moments later in the walk-in pantry playing with the potatoes.

Despite the fact Brayden stops my heart from beating several times a day, and I'm sure he is the reason for a few new grey hairs on my head, I wouldn't trade becoming a father for anything.

A life I once thought condemned by the wrong decision is now a life I will do anything to protect.

***

With Brayden sitting comfortably on my hip, I stand in the middle of his bedroom, pointing out different stars and planets in the painted mural on his ceiling and walls. 'What's that?' I ask over-enthusiastically, which just happens to be the universal speak-to-your-child tone of voice.

He smiles and replies with 'star' while simultaneously clapping his hands because he knows already that he's correct.

'Good boy,' I praise him, holding out my fist for him to bump. He playfully obliges, but misses my hand entirely, inevitably punching me in the chest. 'And what's that?' I ask again, pointing to the moon.

'Star,' he repeats, again clapping himself cheerily. Everything that is painted on the walls around us, to Brayden, is a star.

Not wanting my son to start his astronomy education with the wrong information, I correct him as per usual. 'No, Bray. That's the moooooon,' I say, practically mooing like a friggin' cow.

He giggles at my stupidity and watches my lips intently as I sound the word. His concentration level amazes me, together with just how much information he absorbs at such a young age. Brayden — just like his older siblings — is shaping up to be another little human sponge.

'Bryce, where's Brayden? He'd better be with you,' Alexis calls out from downstairs. 'And he'd better be dressed. Everyone will be here soon.'

Turning toward the door, the direction from which Alexis' bellowing came, I get a playful idea. 'Can you hear Mummy? Should we hide from her? Yeah. Come on, little man, let's play hide-and-seek.'

I look around the room for a hiding place to initiate some secret Daddy business. Then, walking quickly toward the curtains, I position us behind them, not doing a very good job of completely disguising our whereabouts.

'Bryce!' Alexis calls out again, this time sounding more agitated.

'Mummy is getting grumpy,' I tell Brayden.

'Mum mum mum,' he chants in response while poking me in the cheek. Brayden — just like his mother — loves my stubble. Charli ... not so much.

Chuckling like a childish idiot, I kiss him on the head. 'Sh, you'll give us away.'

'Bryce, where are yo—' Alexis says with exasperation, stepping into the room and cutting her words short. I'm guessing her reason being due to spotting our not very inconspicuous hiding spot.

Brayden, hearing his mother's voice, blurts out her name. 'Mum.'

I shake my head, silently laughing to myself. *What the fuck are you doing behind this curtain, you fool?*

Using her mummy-baby voice, Alexis responds. 'What was that? Did I just hear BB?'

Bloody BB, I hate that name.

'BB,' Brayden repeats, forcing a giggle from Alexis.

'I did hear BB! Where is he? Is he under his cot? Nooo. Is he in his toy box? Nooo.'

Hearing her voice get closer and closer with each word that she says, I, along with Brayden, now find myself getting excited in anticipation of her discovering us. *Seriously, how old am I?*

'Where could he be? I know,' she taunts, the curtain now the only thing separating us from her. 'Is he behind the curtain?' Alexis asks, as she gently pokes Brayden in the leg.

He squeals with excitement before she wrenches the curtain aside, revealing our secret Daddy business.

'There you are!' she exclaims.

The look on each of their faces is priceless, their eyes glimmering at each other with elation, their beaming smiles stabbing my heart with a knife forged from love.

'Were you hiding from Mummy? Come here, cheeky boy.' She puts her arms out and, instantly, Brayden lunges toward them. 'Your daddy is naughty,' she says while giving me a sexy grin.

Naughty is one description that fits my current state; another is turned-on and hard as a fucking rock.

Alexis turns away, and I watch with greedy eyes as she sets Brayden down on the floor with his toy cars. The tight-fitting navy dress she has chosen to wear today hugs her body in the right places, sculpting her arse with perfect precision as she bends over.

Swallowing dryly while blood flows from the head on my shoulders to the head on my dick, I adjust my now swelling cock in my pants and map out in my head how I am going to relieve the aching throb underneath my hand.

Visuals of the many ways I can bury myself in between her legs start to filter into my head.

'Okay, sweetheart, you play vroom-vroom while Mummy gets your clothes out,' Alexis says before making her way into Brayden's closet.

Not wanting to waste this perfect opportunity to corner and seduce her, I immediately close and lock Brayden's bedroom door, then follow her into the walk-in wardrobe. As I step into the doorway, I find her stretching on her tiptoes, trying desperately to reach a box on a higher shelf. My initial instinct is to rake the length of her sexy body with my eyes, finding it almost impossible to look past her legs. When Alexis wears stockings, I know that at the tops of her thighs are thick bands of lace that I want nothing more than to remove with my teeth.

I'm now fully aware of my extensive erection and step right up to her side, purposely pushing it into her hip as I slowly reach the box for her. The moment she registers my wanting hard-on, her eyes widen, and the corners of her mouth lift into a seductive smile.

Alexis' smile is hypnotic ... magnetic even, drawing me into a trance-like state. Unable to look away from her captivating and now heavy-lidded gaze, I reach blindly beside us and place the box down on the tallboy.

'We don't have time,' she whispers unconvincingly as I get right up into her personal space, slowly stepping her backward until she is pressed up against the wall.

'We always have time,' I verify, closing the gap between our lips.

The warm wet taste of her tongue as she slides it against mine sets my body alight, waking up every nerve ending I possess. And, with my patience to have her now at a bare minimum, I reach down and lift her right leg, gripping her thigh and holding it to my hip. My other hand finds her jaw and then trails down her throat until I stop it at the hollow of her neck.

'Mm,' I groan while pressing my cock against her, teasing her with my *solid* promise and making her eyelids flutter.

The top of her cleavage provokes my hand's further descent, my fingers now enjoying their journey across the dips and mounds of her breasts, breasts that for the past three months I have had the pleasure of having my way with. Apparently, Alexis decided to stop feeding Brayden due to something called mass-eye-tits ... mass-tits ... massive tits. *Fuck! I don't know what it was called, but it had something to do with her tits.* Either way, she stopped feeding him and I'm not going to lie — thank fuck that she did. My mouth was starting to get nipple-withdrawal.

Licking my lips to moisten them, I wrench down her dress and bra cup, freeing her breast and watching with delight as it bounces beautifully before settling into my hand. The feel of her soft. plump flesh within my fingers triggers my desperation to tease her hardened nipple with my thumb before bending down and taking it into my mouth.

Alexis' reaction to having her breasts teased, licked and sucked, is one of sheer fucking enjoyment to watch. Her chest always rises with her desperate intake of oxygen, all the while pushing her flesh further into my hand and mouth — I love it.

Relishing her perked, hardened nipple underneath my tongue, I tease and tantalise it, flicking the stiff peak with intensity before sucking and stretching it with my mouth.

'Oh, god!' she moans while clenching my hair and tugging it with ardour.

That moan, that go damn fucking moan.

Growling like the beast that she brings out in me, I reach down, pull her underwear aside and caress her moist skin with my fingertips. 'Alexis, just so you know ...' I breathe heavily into her ear. 'You were made to be touched with my fingers, licked with my tongue and fucked with my cock. Honey, you were made for *ME*.'

Her head drops back with a light thump against the wall, exposing her delectable neck. 'Yes,' she murmurs, her tone sexually intoxicating.

I growl once again before undoing my trousers and releasing my cock, positioning it at her entrance before ploughing the fuck into her. I'm needy, eager and desperate for the feel of her, wanting nothing more than to have that privilege without another second wasted.

Digging my fingertips into the skin of her thigh, and bracing my hand on the wall behind her head, I begin to pound into her.

'Fuck, Bryce,' she breathes out while lifting her head back up.

My eyes lock onto her hungry stare, a stare of raw unconcealed passion that blankets my soul and renders me slave to her every whim, need and desire.

'Vroom, bang!' Brayden playfully shouts, snapping me right the fuck out of pussyland and placing me directly into daddyland. I freeze solid, my cock stunned into immobility.

'Don't you dare stop,' Alexis hisses.

'But Brayden sounds like he's —'

'Bryce Edward Clark! *You* came in here, *you* stalked me like a friggin' hungry lion, *you* and your dirty mouth had me all but coming onto your hand, and now *you* want to stop? Well, screw *you*! Either *you* start that cock of yours back up again and make me sink my teeth into your shoulder, or get the fuck out while *I* finish myself off.'

What. The. Fuck?

I'm speechless, impressed, and completely turned-on by her demanding fiery attitude. 'You want my cock to start up again?' I tease with an eyebrow raised. My cock twitches, prompting her face to light up with her sexy, gorgeous smile.

'Yes,' she demands and rocks her hips back and forth, sliding me in and out of her.

Once again, I feel that sensational build-up of pressure as I brace myself and drag my cock out of her, only to drive it back in, again and again until she is doing what she promised — biting my shoulder and muffling her cries of pleasure.

***

'Whose freakin' idea was this?' Tash exclaims as she steps into the apartment. 'I know it's a first birthday party and all, but seriously ... you have gone absolutely overkill with the damn balloons.'

I shrug my shoulders at her, as if to say I had absolutely no part in it when truth be told, I knew all along we were practically filling the joint with helium-inflated latex orbs.

Alexis had decided this was the perfect payback for Tash's antics a few weeks back, when Tash had deliberately staged a fake security alert while Alexis took Brayden out shopping. Apparently Tash thought it would be hilarious to pretend Alexis was European royalty, following her around the shopping precinct like a highly trained bodyguard, except she kept speaking a language that did not exist. Needless to say, Alexis ended up cutting her shopping trip short and has been patiently awaiting her moment of retribution.

'Overkill, Taaaash?' Alexis drawls. 'Surely these few balloons are not going to hurt you,' she adds, while picking one up.

'Alexis, whatever you are contemplating, don't!' Tash warns, pointing her finger with a resolute stab. 'I mean it, missy, you come any closer with that balloon and I will lose my shit and haunt you in the afterlife.'

Alexis smiles a devilishly sweet retort and gestures toward the lounge area. 'I don't know what you are talking about. Please, come in and enjoy your afternoon,' she says as she gently serves the balloon in the air and whacks it with her hand tennis-style.

Tash flinches, glares at her, and hesitantly walks past, now in search of Brayden who is playing with his cousin Alexander on the rug.

I wrap my arm around Alexis' shoulder. 'You enjoyed that, didn't you?'

She tries to restrain her laugh. 'You have no idea. And there's plenty more where that came from.'

'Remind me never to cross you.'

'Don't cross me. Or you'll end up in the throes of passion with Krusty the Clown.'

'You're evil at times, you know that?'

'Sucks to be you and have a phobia.'

'Well, everyone is scared of something, even you.'

Alexis bites the inside of her cheek momentarily, then lets go and answers flippantly. 'Nope, not me.'

Leaning in, I whisper into her ear, 'I don't believe you, my love. So guess who is about to dust off his creepy research skills.'

She turns to face me and brushes her lips with mine. 'Dust away, Mr Clark. I know one thing for sure, though ... you don't scare me.'

Before I met Alexis, I was never one to have many gatherings in my home. Sure, I'd invite the boys over for dinner and jam sessions. And Lucy and Nic were always welcome, no matter what time of the day or night. But that was about it. My home was my private space, my sanctuary and kept out of the public eye.

Standing here today, beer in hand, and watching our friends and family enjoy each other's company, I couldn't be more comfortably happy. The seclusion I'd once given myself was now gone, never to return. I'd finally found my purpose in life ... *my* purpose, not a charitable cause, or a brotherly responsibility. My purpose was Alexis and the family we have created. They were now my reason for existence.

'Bryce,' Nate's voice sounds from beside me. 'Mum said it's time for a speech and to cut the cake.'

'Not a problem, buddy. Where's your sister?'

'Playing Twister. Ha ... that rhymes! My sister is playing Twister.'

I can't help laughing at his wit. For a nine year old, the kid is quick. *Shit! Did I just rhyme, too?*

'Can you go tell Charli it's time for cake? I just need to have a quick word with your Uncle Jake.'

Before I even have a second to process what I just said, Nate bursts into laughter. 'Cake and Jake,' he cackles uncontrollably. 'Good one!' *Ah, bloody hell!*

I playfully turn him around and lightly shove him in the direction of Charlotte. 'Go, you crazy kid!'

Shaking my new-found Dr Seuss skills out of my head, I find Jake by the pool with Graeme. 'Got a minute?' I ask him. 'Actually, you both could probably help me.'

'I don't want her back,' Graeme announces. 'She's yours, you wanted her. You can't give her back.'

'You're a funny man, Graeme. But I wouldn't give Alexis back for the world,' I honestly say.

'Good. As much as I love her, I'm too old for her drama-filled life.'

I give him a reassuring squeeze on the shoulder. 'Rest assured, I'm keeping her.'

'I always thought you were a crazy fucker,' Jake pipes in as he takes a swig of his beer. 'From that moment Lex and Jen told me you were flying around the farm in your helicopter, I thought you were cracked.'

I laugh at Jake's stab and give him a *very* firm, manly slap on the back, causing him to choke on some of his beer. 'Thanks, mate. So, I need to know what Alexis is afraid of. She tells me nothing, but that's just bullshit.'

'Spiders,' they both say simultaneously.

Jake then chuckles. 'Big, fat, furry, spiders ... huntsman and wolf spiders, to be exact.'

'You'd think she would be used to them after growing up on a farm,' Graeme adds, while shaking his head in mild disappointment. 'But I guarantee, if one just happened to be in close proximity now, she'd scream the place down.'

'Spiders ... really?' I ponder. 'I thought she just didn't like them.'

Jake slaps my back in return and steps away. 'She doesn't, she bloody *hates* them.'

I smile to myself and tip my beer to my lips, while eye-fucking Alexis with a scheming smirk.

'Whatever it is you are planning on doing, Bryce, don't!' Graeme warns, interrupting my train of thought. 'I'm serious, I don't want her back. And that look you have on your face tells me that could quite possibly be an option.'

***

Gently tapping a spoon on the side of my glass, I indicate to the room that we want quiet to make an announcement.

'Star!' Brayden squeals and claps himself while pointing to his big, yellow, smiley-faced, star birthday cake. He leans forward in order to grab it.

'No, not yet, sweetheart. In a minute,' Alexis reassures him while securing him tightly to her hip.

'Just quickly, before Brayden loses patience and attempts to plough headfirst into his cake, we want to say thanks for coming and celebrating this little man's first birthday with us —' I am about to continue when I hear Charli behind me, making a racket. Turning around, I spot her dragging her karaoke machine into position.

'Charlotte, what are you doing?' Alexis whispers.

'I want to sing Brayden a song.'

I subdue a smile with pursed lips and make eye contact with Alexis. She too hides her grin. 'Oh ... okay.' She turns back around and addresses the room. 'Um ... apparently Charli has a little something she wants to share.'

'I want to sing "Happy Birthday" to Brayden,' Charli announces just a bit too loudly into the microphone, sending a high-pitched tone throughout the room. 'He is the best brother, ever!' she continues while squinting her eyes and poking her tongue out at Nate.

Alexis slaps her hand to her forehead.

Brayden lunges for the cake again.

Nate smacks a balloon into Charlotte's head.

Tash screeches and dodges its rebound.

Charlotte growls.

And ... I just laugh.

***

After Charli performs her entertaining version of 'Happy Birthday', Alexis and I decide to inform everyone of our decision to get married in six months.

'Oh, and one last *minor* detail,' I express playfully, receiving an elbow to the ribs from Alexis. 'We have finally set a date for the wedding! Mark out February fourth on your calendars.'

'About time!' Tash calls out from her position at the bifold doors, the furthest spot from the balloons.

'There's still time to change your mind, Bryce,' Jake calls out, Johanna snorting in response.

Rick and Claire step up to us, Claire smiling meekly while Rick embraces Alexis. Months ago, I would have wanted to punch the fucker for being this close to her.

'Congratulations! Sorry, but we really need to head off. RJ has his soccer semi-final later today,' Rick explains before they make an early departure.

Approximately one month ago, Rick informed Alexis that he and Claire were expecting a child. Alexis — not surprisingly — took the news really well, being genuinely happy for the two of them. Charlotte had refused — and still refuses to this day — to accept that her next sibling would be anything other than a girl. And Nate just carried on as if an extra baby coming into his life was nothing new. Seeing all three of them react with pleasant attitudes, I decided there and then to let go of my grudge and anger toward Rick. If Alexis was happy, then so was I.

Re-entering the lounge area after seeing Claire and Rick out, we are both smothered by Maryann with congratulatory hugs. 'Wonderful. I can't wait. We need to sit down and start planning —'

'Mum, back off. You know what happened last time you interfered with wedding plans,' Jen cautions.

'Yeah, well ... your sister isn't as mean as you. She wouldn't make me wear a stupid t-shirt to her hen's night, would you, Alexis darling?' Maryann says with gag-worthy sweetness.

Alexis rolls her eyes at her mother's attempt at buttering her up. 'Actually, I'm not having a hen's night.'

'Like fun you aren't,' Carly interjects. 'Trust me, you are having one whether you are in attendance or not.'

'Carly, we've decided to just have a get-together here.' I add, taking Brayden from Alexis. 'Set up the band ... that sort of thing.'

'Not gonna happen, mate,' Derek implies as he raises his beer. 'Consider yourself havin' a buck's night.'

Alexis turns to face me, drops her head on her my shoulder and closes her eyes.

'Ake up, Mum,' Brayden shouts, Wiggles style.

Alexis grumbles with a laugh. 'Mummy isn't sleeping like Jeff.'

'Ake up, Mum,' he hollers, again.

We all laugh.

CHAPTER FIFTEEN

Five months down the track, and it is decided that yes, we are having a hen's night and a buck's night. It is also decided — not by us, mind you — that Carly and Derek are in charge of the entire event.

The plan is to start off together at Opals as one big group, where Live Trepidation will dedicate their entire set to Alexis and play all of her favourite songs. Then we are to go our separate ways, and what will follow is unknown to the both of us. That minor detail I did not like. I didn't like it at all.

***

'I can't believe we agreed to this,' Alexis mumbles from our walk-in wardrobe.

I'm standing in the bathroom, latching the buckle on my denim jeans and fastening the last button on my short-sleeved, light grey shirt. 'We didn't really have a choice, honey. Did you want to argue with Carly *and* Derek?'

'No,' she groans. 'Hey! Maybe we could just stay at Opals together? Refuse to leave?' she suggests, a spark of renewed hope sounding in her voice.

'Yeah, don't think that is going to work.'

I finish off with a little gel in my hair and step out into our bedroom to put on my shoes. Sitting on the edge of the bed and bending over, I slide my foot into the black loafer. Before I can reach for the other shoe, I notice two black high heels only centimetres from my feet.

'Can you zip me up, please?' Alexis asks.

I travel the length of her legs until I'm looking up at her with my mouth and eyes wide open. She is wearing an extremely short black lace dress, which reveals quite a lot of her silky smooth skin, more skin than I'm willing to share the sight of with any other man. And even though she looks as sexy as hell, I'll be damned if she is going to look that good so that some loser can discreetly blow a load in his pants.

'What is that?' I ask on a choke.

'What's what?' she asks, quickly glancing toward the roof where she thinks I am looking, her expression indicating she expects to see some type of critter.

'What you're wearing.'

Alexis looks back down and smooths out her dress. 'Um ... I think it's Dolce and Gabbana. I can check if you wan—'

'I don't fucking care who designed it.'

Her face contorts. 'You don't like it?'

Placing my hands on her legs, I pull her toward me. 'Honey, you look sensational, too fucking sensational. It's just ...' I lean back on the bed and run my hand through my hair. *Fuck, she looks irresistible.* 'I'm not going to be with you all night. You can't wear that without me.'

Climbing over my lap and straddling me on the bed, a sly grin creeps across her face. 'Are you telling me what I can and can't wear?'

'Yes, you seriously can't wear that. Remember that time you called me Jackie Chan?'

She screws up her face, then smiles. 'Yeah.'

'Well, I'll be performing Jackie Chan's all night if you wear that.'

Alexis laughs and leans forward, her golden blonde locks cascading around her face as she looks down at me. Even her lips are turning me on — red as a friggin' fire truck.

'Bryce, I'm a big girl. I can take care of myself. And anyhow, we have the apartment to ourselves tonight. Don't you want to wait till we get home so that you can take this dress off and see just exactly what I'm wearing underneath?'

I glance down at her breasts, spying the tiniest hint of red lace covering her chest. *Bloody hell!*

'Fuck the night out. Let's stay here and you can show me now.'

I reach for her tits, but she jumps off and puts her hand up. 'No. We are going. Now, can you please zip me up?'

Alexis turns around, baring her back to me and giving me another sneak peek of her lingerie. The sight of her red corset prompts my dick to stand at attention, poised and motionless, saluting her military-style. Having no choice but to close my eyes in order to try and gather my not so turned-on composure, I lower my eyelids and click my neck from side to side.

After a second of thinking about Dame Edna Everage — because let's face it, she looks like a clown — I reopen them to find Alexis still standing in front of me, her head now turned back in my direction and smiling from ear to fucking ear.

Completely depleted of all willpower and restraint, I grab a hold of her and drag her to the bed, pinning her down underneath me. 'Honey, if you are going to wear that, then first I need to fuck you. I need you wearing me along with it.'

***

Alexis and I walk into Opals nearly three-quarters of an hour late, spotting our friends and family scattered around the dance floor. Will, Matt, Derek and Luce are up on stage, preparing for our gig.

'Sorry we are late,' Alexis apologises, blushing profusely.

Carly's eyes widen as they journey up and down Alexis' body. 'No need to explain why. That,' she points to her outfit, 'speaks for itself.'

'What? There's nothing wrong with my dress,' Alexis whines while Tash hands her a drink and a condom-decorated veil. 'Oh, for the love of god ... I am not wearing that! I'm not in my twenties and getting married for the first time. FOR. GET. IT.'

'Told you she wouldn't wear it,' Tash says to Carly, handing her the veil.

'She'll wear it ... give it time ... and alcohol.'

I shake my head, kiss Alexis, and hoist myself up on the stage.

'Nice of you to show, arsehole,' Derek throws my way as I pick up my guitar and begin to tune it.

'I was busy,' I answer, pulling a pick out of my jeans pocket.

'Hmm, yeah ... I can see why,' Matt murmurs, glancing toward Alexis.

'Shut up, dick. I already have to worry about every other sleaze in this joint eye-fucking my fiancée. I don't want to have to worry about you, too.'

'She looks hot!' Lucy says with her back to me.

I turn to my sister. 'Not you, too,' I grimace.

'No. I didn't mean it like that ... although, she does look hot!'

Will laughs as he taps out a light beat.

'Let's just get started, yeah?' I grumble as I glance toward Alexis, taking in the smouldering beauty that she is. I can't say that I really blame them for fucking around with me, she does look exceptionally incredible tonight. And as I watch her greet her family and friends, it painfully dawns on me that my night is not going to be as laidback as hers. Not in the bloody slightest!

We open the show with 'Birth' by 30STM, just like we had at our previous gig. The song is a crowd-pleaser and, quite frankly, a great intro to get everyone — including us — primed for the rest of our gig.

Three songs into our set we decide to play one of our own: 'Chaos'. This particular song seems to sum up my current situation, since during the second bridge I have no choice but to be witness to a group of guys eyeing Alexis, Carly and Jen.

Highly fucking irritated, I watch as the group of douche bags spend a minute planning their approach, the shady thoughts in their minds quite obviously radiating from their over-zealous faces.

Cringing like fuck when they slowly make their way toward the girls, I notice Tash and Steve intercept the group's attempted pick-up, Steve spinning Jen into a dance and Tash wrapping herself around Alexis in a bear hug, pretending to give her a friendly cuddle. I inwardly sigh with relief at the fact I no longer have to jump off the stage and threaten to jam my guitar down any of the guys' throats. Being that Opals is my nightclub, I really don't want to cause a scene.

Tash gives the four guys a vicious snarl, then looks toward me and winks, and I can't help smirking with the knowledge of our agreement that she will be Alexis' bodyguard. Now, it's not as if I formulated this understanding behind Alexis' back. In fact — if I remember rightly — Tash and I discussed our intentions directly in front of her years back when we watched the kids swim at school. So, technically, it is not my, nor Tash's, fault that she did not take us seriously.

After finishing the song and realising I'm going to need more protective reinforcements, I give Dale — my head of security — a quick call.

'Everything all right, mate?' he answers.

'Yeah. Listen, Dale, before you finish and make your way down here, can you send Joey. I need him on Alexis-duty tonight.'

I imagine Dale running his hands over his face in frustration at my request.

'She's not gonna be happy when she catches on, Bryce, and you know she will.'

'Do me a favour. Turn on Opal's lower dance floor camera. You can't miss her. Then tell me I'm going overboard.'

I wait for him to do what I've just directed him to do, anticipating that he is now on my wavelength.

'Right! Yep, I get ya. Joey will be there as soon as possible.'

'Good. Now turn the camera off, you dirty perve.'

He laughs. 'It's off. I know better than to mess with you.'

'So you should. I'll see you shortly.'

'No worries.'

I hang up the phone and turn back to face the crowd, even more pissed off to see the numbers practically doubling. What shits me further is that the male to female ratio is not in my favour. I don't fucking need any more dick-heavy men in Alexis' proximity.

'Bryce, you ready now?' Derek asks, looking annoyed.

I hold up my finger. 'Just give me a minute.'

Before we begin our next song, I quickly call Lisa who is on door-entry this evening.

'Opals Nightclub, Lisa speaking.'

'Lisa, it's Mr Clark.'

'Oh, yes, sir. How can I help you?'

'Tell whoever is manning the door that the ratio is off. Limit the men for the next hour, then get them to do another assessment.'

'Sorry, sir. I will tell Tony now.'

'Good. Thank you, Lisa.'

I hang up the phone once again and find Alexis watching me, concern on her face. Wanting to ease her mind, I make my way to the edge of the stage and squat down.

'What's wrong, honey?'

'You look agitated. Is everything all right?'

'Yes, everything is fine. I just had to arrange a few things.'

'Okay, but this is your buck's night, too. I want you to enjoy yourself.'

'I will,' I reassure her, lightly tapping her nose with my finger. 'But first I want to watch your reaction to the next song.'

She smiles that earth-shattering smile I love so much. 'Ooh, what is it?'

Waggling my eyebrows at her, I stand up. She runs her tongue along the top row of her teeth while her eyes travel the length of my jeans. It has me wanting to abandon the night and take her back to our apartment.

'Alexis,' I growl in warning, her look indicating her inner salacious thoughts.

'What? I'm waiting,' she shouts in response, now smiling innocently.

I'll give her waiting.

Before nodding toward Lucy to begin the song, I notice Joey enter the room. I acknowledge him with a swift lift of my chin as he proceeds to stand not too far from Alexis' position. Just having him here now puts my mind at ease a little.

Taking another step back, I wink at Luce, and just like the time we played in Shepparton she and Derek are the only ones illuminated by light as she begins to play the piano in 'November Rain' by Guns N' Roses.

Alexis — standing at the very front of the stage — blows a kiss in my direction, cementing the fact that I was right when choosing to re-enact this performance for her. I knew she'd love it.

Just like that time, when I performed this song to Alexis with the sole message that I would wait as long as it took for her to realise that we were perfect for each other, I once again serenade her during the guitar solos, even showing off and kissing her passionately while still playing like the freak that I am.

I'm normally not one to show off or flaunt my talents and wealth like an unappreciative flog and wanker. But playing the guitar is something I'm good at, *really* good at. It's also something that made my father extremely proud of me, and he told me to always go hard at it. And it was because of Dad that I had learned to play in the first place. He had given me lessons from the ripe old age of four, he too being a brilliant musician. Music ran in our family. My grandmother had been a violinist and apparently her aunty had been an opera singer.

When I was ten years old and Lucy six, we used to sit around the lounge room and play our instruments. Mum loved the piano and could voice a fairly good tune, in fact, and we all had a natural love for music, a passion for producing a melodic sound. Those particular memories stood out for me the most, being some of the happiest times in my life.

I, too, want those times for my family. To teach Brayden, Nate and Charli — if they want — to play an instrument. I'd love nothing more than to sit back and listen to them harmonise with each other while Alexis sings. It's one of my family traditions that I hope to uphold.

Finishing off the song and standing on top of the piano as a tribute to Slash, I wink at my woman. The twinkle in her eyes is all

I needed to know that the complete over-the-top act I just displayed was worth it. My sole reason now for playing the guitar on stage ... purely for her. Alexis' reaction is all that matters to me.

'Okay, ladies and gents. We have one final song to play for this evening then we are off to celebrate our leading guitarist's final night out as a bachelor. Yes, ladies, I'm sorry to inform you, but my man, Bryce, in just a few short weeks will be marrying this beautiful lady in front of him,' Derek says boldly, gesturing toward Alexis.

She raises her hands and I nearly have a fit. The dress she is wearing is strapless and should not be worn by someone who raises their hands, especially someone like Alexis. Not knowing what else to do, I jump down off the stage and wrap my arms around her, covering her nearly-exposed breasts.

She happily welcomes my embrace and drapes her hands around my neck. 'Hi.'

'Hi,' I say back, before taking her mouth with my own.

'Oh, all right you two, hurry up,' Derek complains as the crowd wolf-whistles.

I separate my mouth from hers and whisper into her ear. 'As much as I love to see your tits, my love, please keep your hands below shoulder level. No one else needs to see them.'

Kissing her cheek quickly while she gives me a puzzled look, I pull away and climb back on stage. As I turn around, I notice an expression of anger on her face and her arms are now folded across her chest. Before I can jump back down and ask her what's wrong, Lucy and Will begin playing the intro to 'You're the Voice' by John Farnham and I have no choice but to stand there and wonder what the fuck is wrong with her. *I just saved her from flashing the crowd. Surely that's a good thing.*

By the time Derek starts singing the pre-chorus, her frown has disappeared and she is enjoying the song with her friends. In fact, now that I'm no longer focussed on her change of character, I become aware that the entire club is fully engrossed in our performance.

It really shouldn't surprise me. This is, after all, a great song; an iconic song. And it dawns on me, as I take in the patrons swaying and singing along, that I should've bloody ignored Derek and gone with a live bagpipe player. It would've been perfect. *Fucking Derek!*

Winding down the song and playing the coda till the end, I smile and sigh with relief that our set is finally over. As much as I adore playing the guitar — especially for Alexis — I want nothing more than to spend some time wrapped around her gorgeous body. Not only for the sheer fucking delight and feel of her in my arms, but also to shield her from the many sets of perverted eyes I have spotted around the room.

'Thanks guys,' I say to the band. 'She loved it.'

'Glad my percussion talents have assisted in you getting your dick wet tonight,' Will offers as he pats me on the back. 'Now, let's hope they do the same for me.'

He jumps off the stage and heads toward Carly's friend.

'Has Will got a thing goin' on with Carly's friend?' I ask.

'Her name is Libby,' Derek answers. 'And yeah, kind of ... he hopes to, anyway.'

I inwardly smile to myself, enjoying the fact that Will, too, seems to have taken a liking to someone who doesn't resemble an eighteen year-old.

'So where are we headed next?' I ask with not much enthusiasm.

'You'll see. Come on, pack up your axe. We're goin'.'

***

After putting my guitar away, I make my way down from the stage and head toward Alexis. Her back is to me, and her arms are propped on top of a bar table. She is bent over just a little, and I can't help but stare at her legs, especially the one which is gently rubbing up and down the back of her calf muscle.

As I begin to stalk my prey, I am approached by a couple of women.

'You were so good up there,' one of them says with a suspect smile. 'How long have you been playing?'

'Yeah,' the other agrees, 'you should play professionally or something.'

Never being one who enjoyed being hit on, especially by women who have absolutely no idea of what is going on outside of their own little pick-me bubble, I politely give them the brush-off, thanking them for their empty compliments and continuing on my way until I am pressed up against Alexis.

'I want you,' I whisper into her ear.

'Really?' she whispers back. 'Are you sure you just don't want anyone else to want me?' Her icy response is somewhat sulky.

Confused as to what she is implying — because yes, I sure as hell 'don't want anyone else to want her' — I ask her what's wrong. 'Want to tell me why you sound pissed off?'

She tries to shrug out of my arms, which are still firmly wrapped around her waist. I tighten my grip, she isn't going anywhere.

'The only reason you kissed me before in front of everyone was because you didn't want people accidentally seeing a little bit of my skin. And just for your information, I'm wearing Hollywood fashion tape so my "tits" will remain within my dress.'

Not allowing her to dwell on her ridiculousness any further, I spin her around and get right up into her beautiful face. 'Let's get one thing straight. I kiss you because I want to fucking kiss you, because I like it and because you taste good. So don't think for one second that I have an ulterior motive,' I growl on a whisper, as I lean in and get just that bit closer to tasting the lips that required this explanation in the first place. 'And as for your tits, yes, I want them to remain in that dress of yours. They are for my eyes only, honey ... unless ... you have a problem with that?'

Her expression softens and her body become less rigid within my arms. I feel that her resolve is melting away. Leaning in, I remove that final torturous centimetre between us and press my lips to hers, kissing her with as much passion as I'm capable of and holding her head to mine while dipping her in my arms.

When Alexis is secured to me, wrapped around me, completely encompassing everything I possess and breathe, I feel nothing but total satisfaction. She absolutely fulfils me.

'Will you two just get a room,' someone complains, that someone sounding a bit like Lil. 'You have many rooms. Hotels full of rooms, in fact. Go and use one of those for god's sake.'

'Shut up, Lil. Leave them alone. They are getting married soon. Plus, watching them is hot!'

Alexis giggles against my mouth at Jade's argument with Lil then locks eyes with me and smiles. 'They are right,' she says a little louder. 'We should get a room. Actually, we should get one now.' She pulls away from me and straightens her dress before threading her fingers through mine. 'Okay, ladies, thanks for everything. We are calling it a night.'

'Oh no, you're not,' Carly interjects with a determination that is not to be argued with. She storms over to Alexis and prises her hand from mine.

Now, if I really wanted to, I could foil her attempts. The thing is, I have a little something up my sleeve, and his name is Joey, so allowing Alexis to go with her friends is no longer an issue. I know he will protect her and report to me as often as I want him to.

'Fine! Fine! I'm coming,' she groans before turning back and giving me one last kiss. 'Be good.'

I shoot her a half-grin as she's tugged away. 'I'm always good.'

'Where are you taking me?' Alexis complains to Carly and Jen as they link their arms through hers.

'Upstairs. We have a surprise for you,' Jen giggles.

I turn to Derek while watching them skip off. 'What surprise?'

'Want a drink?' he asks, ignoring my question and heading toward the bar.

As I wait for him to come back, I can't help but feel uneasy about Alexis' 'surprise'. I hate not fucking knowing what is going on.

A well-built — and if I'm completely honest — good-looking bloke in a cop's uniform, holding a duffle bag, walks past. His shady appearance is distracting and only adds to my already unsettled frame of mind. Derek returns and sets my beer down on the bar table, and we both follow the cop with our eyes as he disappears from the club.

Confusion settles in as I wonder why a police officer has just strolled through my nightclub, a police officer who looks far too pretty to be a cop. Hearing my phone ring from within my pocket, I pull it out and answer it, not even bothering to look who it is, my bewildered state of mind controlling my actions.

'Sir, Alexis has just entered a suite with her friends. Do you want me to wait outside?' Joey asks.

Agitated and not really paying attention, I tell him he can leave, and then disconnect the call. Moments later, the fog covering my mind seems to lift and I begin to comprehend why I suddenly feel slightly ill.

'Derek, what fucking surprise have they got for Alexis?' I ask again, hoping to god that cop wasn't what I thought he was.

The fucker shrugs his shoulders, but clearly knows what the hell is going to happen upstairs.

'That had better not have been some cockhead, wannabe dancer pretending to be a cop, who wants nothing more than to handcuff my fiancée and place her hands all over his spray-tanned, oily body,' I furiously spit out.

Feeling utterly murderous at the thought of another man forcing her to touch him and touching her in return, I begin to follow in the direction the girls headed.

'No, you don't,' Derek says while restraining me.

'Derek, fuck off! Let me go.'

'Dude, it's just for one night. And anyway, Miss Nude Australia awaits you in villa four,' he says as he releases one hand and waves a room key in my face.

'You're an idiot, a deadset idiot. If you think for one second I am going to choose some stripper over rescuing Alexis from some slimy creep, you are dumber than dog shit. Let me go, now!'

'What's goin' on?' Will asks as he steps up to the both of us, assessing Derek's armlock hold.

'Pansy here wants to ditch Nude Australia and act all caveman in front of Alexis.'

'Speak fucking English,' Will complains.

'Carly has arranged a stripper for Alexis. I've arranged one for Bryce. Bryce doesn't want to go. The dickhead doesn't want Alexis to go either. I am currently stopping him from ruining everything. Wanna help me out?'

I apply a compression poke to Derek's L11 pressure point, right in the crook of his elbow joint. This is my warning. If he doesn't let me go in the next second, I will do some serious damage.

'Argh! Fuck, Bryce. Will, a little help, please.'

Will steps in and restrains my hands.

'You arseholes! That dancing pretty-boy cop is about to rub his cock all over our women. How you can be all right with that is beyond me.'

'What pretty-boy cop?' Will queries, stepping back and looking confused. 'You mean the one who walked past just before. That big, dark, handsome police officer is a stripper?'

Derek tilts his head to the side in an assessment of Will. 'Are you gay, man? I don't care if you are, each to their own.'

'No, I'm not gay. I'm actually this close,' he says, holding his thumb and pointer finger in Derek's face, 'this bloody close to having Libby touch *my* cock. And I'll be damned if that dancing cop bloke gets his touched before mine. Let him go, Derek.'

'You're weak. Both of you are fucking weak,' Derek spits out as he lets me go.

'What room are they in?' I ask, picking up my pace and heading for the exit.

'Don't know,' Derek calls back with a shit-eating grin.

I stop, turn fully around and start for him. 'Tell me what room they are in or you'll have no teeth left. And I can tell you, a lead singer without teeth will sound pretty fucking hilarious.'

He studies my face for a second. 'You're joking.'

'Am I? Let me ask you something. You've seen how Carly reacts to men, men with big muscles in particular. Imagine how she is going to react to bodybuilder stripper jerk. You sure you're all right with that, all right with her dragging her hands across his chest, clenching his biceps, his arse and feeling his sweaty junk?'

'She won't touch his junk,' he affirms with not much conviction.

'You sure? Perhaps she likes police officers more than firemen.'

I watch him lose the battle of cockiness. 'Shit! Motherfucking shit!'

'Which room?' I ask for the last time.

'Presidential suite two,' he surrenders.

Not wasting a second longer, I sprint for the elevator, Derek and Will not far behind me.

'If I walk in and see that naked fucker at full mast, thrusting it in Alexis' face, I will kill you,' I say, glaring at Derek as I swipe my card through the security lock on the presidential suite's door.

Will laughs. 'You're a fool, man,' he says sympathetically as he pats Derek on the back. 'I can't believe you thought you'd get away with this.'

'I'm glad you find this funny, Will. You just wait until you find a woman who you can't get out of your head. A woman you will go to the ends of the earth to be with and protect. A woman who becomes your sole reason for breathing. You just wait, mate. Your day will come, and when it does, I will laugh right back at you,' I say as I open the door.

'You're a poetic fucker, aren't you?' Derek teases.

I'm at the point of performing my own chokehold on my best friend, just to knock him out and shut him the hell up, when Justin Timberlake's 'SexyBack' sounds from within the suite.

'Fuck!' I growl, turning to my idiot best friend. Before taking off in the direction of the music and squealing women, I shove Derek so hard that his back hits the wall.

He laughs at me and starts singing along with JT.

With my heart thumping in my chest over what horrid sight I think I'm about to see, I reluctantly turn the corner. Firstly, I lay my eyes on the massive oily bastard who is straddling Alexis' lap as if he is some fucking rodeo star. She is sitting on a single chair in the middle of the room with her friends standing around in a circle, clapping, dancing and raising their champagne-filled glasses in the air. It really is quite ridiculous and bloody nauseating.

My vision goes back to Alexis who — thank god — has her eyes closed and her hands covering her face, clearly not wanting the dickhead treating her like a horse. My heartbeat calms a little, and all I want to do now is rescue her from her apparent distress.

'Hey! Get out!' Carly yells, pointing in my direction. 'No grooms allowed ... unless,' she wiggles playfully, 'you want to start removing your clothes.'

'You ...' I point to her. 'You and I are going to have some words later. 'And you,' I point to the hairless Chippendale wannabe, 'back the fuck off.'

He steps aside with a knowing expression, as though this is not the first time an irate partner has stormed into the room. Alexis sits frozen, a terrified expression on her face, as I stop right beside her chair and tower over her.

She starts to speak, seemingly to defend herself. 'I didn't know —'

Cutting off her unnecessary apology, I reach forward and take hold of her hand, pulling her up to my chest and pressing my lips to hers in a forceful show of ownership. My intention is to make a clear point that she is mine.

Keeping the kiss brutally short, I pull away. 'Want to go home?'

She smiles and nods.

Not wanting to stay any longer and listen to JT sing about being someone's slave, I bend down, throw her over my shoulder — making sure I cover her arse with her dress — and walk us out of the room.

***

When we get back to the apartment, I take the elevator all the way to the second floor, not uttering a word until we are beside the bed.

Before I place her down, I feel her fingers playing with the waistband of my jeans from behind my back.

'Are you mad?' she asks, almost timidly.

'Yep,' I honestly reply, closing my eyes while trying to calm my raging fury together with my raging hard-on which is a result of her teasing touch.

She dips her finger into my jeans, along the crevice of my arse. 'Are you angry with me?'

'No, not with you,' I sigh. 'With our ex-best friends.'

Straightening her back, she encourages me to slide her down my front. 'Good,' she replies with a promising grin, continuing to slide all the way down to her knees. Then, unlatching my belt buckle, she doesn't hesitate in taking me in her hands. 'Because the only man I want dancing around me is you. The only man I want, period, is you.'

Smirking down at her, I caress her stunning face. 'I'm all yours, honey.'

CHAPTER SIXTEEN

My breath catches when I spot her walk out onto the balcony. I can't see her in detail as I am too far away, but her body, adorned in an ivory gown, is unmistakable. I know they say seeing the bride before the wedding is bad luck, but technically, I can't see her entirely. She is several hundred metres away in the distance.

Hoping that she has her phone with her, I pull out my mobile and send her a text:

29 minutes and 13 seconds ~ Bryce

I'll admit it. I'm desperate and unable to help myself needing some form of contact. Spending last night without her was agony. So much so, I was highly fucking tempted to sneak into our apartment and surprise her in the middle of the night. I'm sure she wouldn't have minded. Maryann, however, would have. My prospective mother-in-law would no doubt have physically removed me from the premises — or at least tried.

Watching and waiting for Alexis to answer my message, I notice someone, who looks to be Lucy, join her on the balcony. She hands her what I assume is her phone, which makes me smile boldly. Damn, I adore my sister. She has been the perfect accomplice in my quest for ultimate attainment.

Lucy heads back inside, so I take the opportunity to send another text:

28 minutes, 19 seconds and counting until
you make me the happiest man alive ~ Bryce

ATTAINMENT

I wait, knowing that she is now reading it, and the fact I am watching her without her knowledge leaves me feeling somewhat cocky and powerful at the same time.

My phone beeps, indicating her response:

27 minutes and 21 seconds
until I become Mrs Alexis Clark ~ Alexis

As I read her reply, the smile that covers my face is enormous. Mrs Alexis Clark. It sounds perfect.

I can't wait. ~ Bryce

Neither can I ~ Alexis

Smiling like an impish fool, I figure I'll play with her a little longer, loving to wind her up and watch her unleash her inner warrior. The fight she puts up when returning my challenges always ignites a fiery passion within me.

Well then hurry up ~ Bryce

I love you, you know ~ Alexis

I do ~ Bryce

Aren't you supposed to say that in 25 minutes and 33 seconds
~ Alexis

I laugh out loud. She never fails to amaze me with her wit and responses.

'What are you laughing at, dick?' Derek says from behind as he steps up beside me.

'None of your business,' I reply as I send another message, this one sure to get her excited.

> That's it! I'm coming up there to get you ~ Bryce

'Is that Alexis? Up there on your balcony?'

I look up to my penthouse, still smiling, captivated by her angelic form. 'Sure is.'

'You're unfuckingbelievable. You're not supposed to see her before the ceremony.'

'I can't really see her, not closely enough anyway.'

'Sure, keep tellin' yourself that.'

My phone beeps once more:

> Okay, okay. I'm on my way ♥ ~ Alexis

'Are you texting her?' Derek asks, incredulously.

A sly grin replaces my smile as I continue to type. 'Yep,' I answer with nonchalance.

> You better be ♥ ~ Bryce

'Does she know you are watching her?'

'Of course not.'

'You're a dog, Bryce,' he says as he turns to face me with his back against the railing, trying to block my view.

I raise an eyebrow at the cocky fucker I call my best friend. 'I'm not a dog. I just like to know what she's doing. Get out of the way.' I move him aside and smile once again. 'And anyway, you can't stand there and tell me you aren't well and truly under Carly's thumb.'

'I'm under no one's thumb.'

'Bullshit! Carly owns you.'

'Carly's not like that.'

'It doesn't matter if she's like that or not. You're thumbed ... whipped ... you belong to her. You might as well man the fuck up and admit it.'

'Never, that will never happen.'

'Brayden, come here! Uncle Snakey needs to put your shoes on,' Jake bellows from inside the suite.

I hear Brayden squeal then crack the shits. 'No shoes!'

'Uncle Snakey?' Derek mouths, amusement on his face.

I smile and nod. 'Yep, but don't ask.'

Derek pushes off the railing and heads back inside. 'Come on, man. Let's get you married.'

Taking one last look up at Alexis, who is now hugging her father, I lift my phone and snap a photo. My creepy research is still very much operational.

***

Impatiently waiting at the altar for Alexis, my palms are sweaty and my body tense. I seriously need to rein my shit in, having no doubt that I must look like a nervous wreck. It wouldn't surprise me if I've cracked my neck and clenched my fists more times than a pro boxer would before a fight.

Taking a deep breath, I calm my nerves and watch with amusement as Nate follows Brayden around, making sure he doesn't untie any more of the ivory-ribboned bows decorating the large bunches of roses. Seriously, the amount of destruction my son can get up to in the blink of an eye still confounds me.

'Nervous?' Jessica enquires as she steps up to my side. *Nervous? Yeah, if my damp friggin' hands are anything to go by, I'm very bloody nervous.*

'No, not at all,' I lie, leaning forward and giving her a quick kiss on the cheek.

'Hmm,' she responds with a knowing smile. 'Listen, dear. I just want to let you know that your parents and Lauchie ... even Gareth, are all here in spirit. They are proud of you. We all are.'

I manage a small smile and give her a hug. 'Thank you.'

'You're welcome.' She pulls away, gives my arm a quick reassuring squeeze and then finds her seat.

As I contemplate what she just said, Maryann approaches. Her demeanour is both excited and anxious. 'She's just outside,' she explains.

Feeling my pulse pick up a beat, I look toward the door, noticing Alexis' bridesmaids lining up ready to walk down the aisle. 'Bray, Nate, come here,' I call to the boys. Nate grabs Brayden's hand and they make their way over. 'Okay, Mum is just outside those doors. Nate, come stand next to me just like we practised.' He does as he's told. 'Now, little man, see your special pillow,' I say to Brayden as I bend down to his eye level. 'I want you to hold it tightly and go with Nanny, okay?' I hold out my fist for him to bump.

He rears his hand back and then slams it into mine. 'Bang!' he says and then laughs, our fist-bumps now being a playful game to him.

Maryann takes his hand and leads him along the aisle and, just as she reaches the door, I catch a glimpse of Alexis. The sight of her, as per usual, steals what oxygen I have left in my lungs. *Fuck!*

The first thing my overwhelmed mind deciphers is that I'm marrying her today. *I'm marrying her today. I'm* really *marrying her today.*

Completely stunned, and spellbound by her presence, I can't help but start to mentally count my blessings. You see, I've lost a lot in my life, suffering heartache and accepting the fact that I was destined — and deserved — to be alone in love. Don't get me wrong ... yes, I've managed to build a hugely successful business and brand, and I never take my fortune for granted. It's just that ever since Alexis came into my life, I've learned how to truly aspire. I've learned to love, and to live life as it should be lived. And it is for this reason that I will be forever grateful.

Sucking in a deep breath, I properly absorb for the first time since walking into this room that today is my wedding day. Today — after a few years of sharing my life with the woman of my dreams — is the day she becomes my wife. This day is the fucking icing on the cake — the pièce de résistance. This day cements what

I have known all along: that Alexis is mine and that she always will be.

Maryann passes Brayden to Alexis and my heart skips a beat as it usually does when I see them together. Watching Alexis and our son interact with one another does things to me that I never thought possible. For one, I can't take my eyes off them, and secondly, I can't help smiling like the fuckin' Joker.

Brayden points in my direction and both he and Alexis hit me with two earth-shattering smiles, smiles that — like hundreds of times before — pierce through me like a bolt of lightning. According to everyone in our life, Brayden looks like me and I must admit, I tend to agree. *The force is strong in my family.* The thing is, he may be a mini-me, but the beam that plasters his eighteen-month-old face is 100% his mother's.

Alexis places Brayden on his stubby little legs. He grabs hold of Maryann's hand and begins to walk toward me. It's in this moment that I finally understand why Alexis wanted to wait two years to get married. She'd pleaded and convinced me the wait would be worthwhile. 'Charli will be at my side and Nate at yours,' she'd said. 'Brayden will then walk down the aisle holding the rings on a cute little pillow ... it will make the day perfect. Please can we wait. I'm not going anywhere, remember?'

I knew that she wasn't going anywhere, that wasn't the point. The point was we were together and had a child of our own; therefore I wanted to be able to call her my wife. So giving in to her pleas had almost killed me, especially after what we had both been through. Waiting was the absolute last fucking thing I had wanted, instead wanting to marry her as soon as I possibly could. After all, I had waited my whole life for her.

Without admitting it to her though, she was right. Watching Brayden as he walks down the aisle toward me is definitely well worth the wait. It's perfect ... the kids are perfect ... Alexis is perfect.

Brayden stops and smiles, obviously pleased with his 'special job'. I bend down and hold my fist out to him, preparing for another right-hook. He indulges me and laughs, then sits down with Maryann.

As the music kicks in, I quickly stand back up and watch Alexis slowly make her way toward me. I'd been picturing and dreaming about this very moment for years, and now it's finally happening. In my dreams, Alexis was angelic ... beautiful ... exquisite. But in reality, watching as she smiles at our family and friends with each step that she takes, she is just pure perfection — fucking breathtaking.

The instrumental musical piece that is playing as she walks down the aisle is one that Lucy, the boys and I composed especially for this moment. We'd spent months on it, making it flawless. I sneak a look over at Derek and watch as he performs an air guitar action, prompting Carly to laugh at him. *Friggin' show pony.*

Shaking my head in amusement, I roll my eyes with a smile. He is definitely whipped whether he admits it or not.

Alexis stops and has a few moments with Graeme. Part of me envies her having her parents here; I briefly wish mine were here, too. Mum would no doubt be crying happy tears and Dad would be patting her arm. Lauchie and Gareth would be standing right by my side, and the day really would be complete. But, as incredibly perfect as that sounds, it is not how it was meant to be. Fate had other plans, plans I would never understand.

Graeme gives Alexis a quick kiss on the cheek before she turns, faces me, and steps up to the altar. *Fuck me, she is gorgeous.*

'Hi,' she mouths, her lips moving seductively yet with a hint of shyness. *Shiiiit! I want at those lips.*

'Can I kiss her now?' I ask, desperately.

The room erupts into an amused chuckle. *I'm glad you all find it funny. I sure as hell don't.* Frustrated at my lack of control, I clench my fist, then open it again.

'I'm sorry, Mr Clark, not quite yet,' announces the celebrant.

Now, if he wasn't the very man who was going to legally bind me to Alexis for the rest of our lives, I would physically remove him from the room for stopping me from kissing her. He should consider himself lucky.

Fighting to refrain from glaring at him, I move my stare back to the love of my life, finding Alexis staring at me, her beauty-filled blue eyes looking deep into mine. 'I love you,' I mouth, having to do or say something to show her how I feel. Apparently, kissing her in this moment is not allowed.

'I love you, too,' she replies quietly as her gaze drops to assess my suit. The way she takes me in with her eyes nearly snaps my dick to attention — nearly. This is my wedding day after all; I do have some degree of control.

ATTAINMENT

Alexis hands her bouquet of roses to her sister, Jen, then turns back to face me, holding her hands out for me to take hold. *Shit! My palms are still sweaty.*

Wiping them on my trousers as quickly and inconspicuously as I am capable of, I take both her hands in mine. She strokes her thumb across my knuckles and, again, my dick nearly snaps to attention. *Bloody hell!* Alexis will always have the ability to charge me with her touch.

Screw this! I raise her hand to my mouth and kiss her wrist, the smell of her perfume intoxicating me. The fight within me to cease my lips further progression up her arm is excruciating. She smiles lovingly at me and, like a magnet, leans in closer. I want to take her in my arms and merge us into one, but the celebrant clears his throat and begins the ceremony.

After exchanging rings and confirming that I never owned my heart to begin with, my heart having always belonged to Alexis, I am now at the absolute end of my tether. I need to kiss her. I need to taste her. I need to feel her in my arms.

With desperation now plaguing my mind, body and soul, I mentally give the celebrant a nice big 'fuck you' and take her in my arms before he has a chance to finish pronouncing us husband and wife. I kiss her like I've never kissed her before. I finally kiss my wife.

CHAPTER SEVENTEEN

Our reception celebrations are a small affair, which we decided to have in one of the function rooms at City Towers. Alexis wanted our entire wedding celebration to be at *our* hotel complex.

As much as I pride myself on our establishment, if Alexis had said that our first night as husband and wife was also going to be in the hotel, I would have probably gagged her. I drew the line at that. Little does she know, we are flying directly to Paris after the wedding reception and I have a few secrets up my sleeve that I can't wait to surprise her with.

***

'Excuse me, ladies and gentleman,' Derek announces through the microphone. 'Can I ask the groom to bring his bride to the dance floor for their first dance as husband and wife?'

Alexis has her head on my shoulder while we sit at our table having a quiet moment to ourselves. As she lifts it up and hits me with, yet again, another dazzling smile, I notice something change in her expression and she gets a look I have seen many times before.

'I hope you are wearing that red G-string, husband,' she drawls.

My eyes widen at her suggestion, and I laugh loudly as I pull her to her feet, leading her to the dance floor. 'It was a one-off, wife. I happily destroyed that uncomfortable piece of arse-floss.'

Placing her hands around my neck, she stands up on her tiptoes to kiss my lips. 'You once told me that nothing was absolute.'

'Some things are,' I say with complete confidence as I return her kiss and wrap my arms around her waist.

A familiar sound filters into my ears when the music begins and I recognise almost instantly, as Derek starts to sing, that he is singing the song I wrote for Alexis, 'Thief of My Heart.'

Pressing her head against my shoulder, she squeezes me tightly. 'Loving you is absolute.'

'It better be,' I say with a smirk.

Alexis pulls away and wipes a tear which has begun to slide down her happy face. 'Bryce, I just want you to know that deciding to go back to work three years ago was one of the best decisions I have ever made.' Another tear leaves her eye, heading on a journey south.

'I can't argue with you there,' I agree, wiping it away.

'Giving you permission to kiss me was another.'

'I married a smart woman.'

She scoffs and drops her head for a second, then looks back into my eyes. 'Spending that week with you and allowing myself to believe that what we had was real, well ... that was another.'

I hug her tightly, thankful that she took that very big leap of faith. Because when I look back on it now, that decision must've have been extremely difficult for her.

Derek picks up the pace, singing the lyrics to the bridge of the song. I too, mouth them to Alexis.

Let go and feel it.
Just let go and feel it.
You and I, we are it.
Please let go.

The timing of those lyrics couldn't be more perfect, emphasising what we had just been talking about. Alexis smiles and sings the chorus back to me.

You're all that I want and nothing else.
I've fallen hard and will never get up.

I swear that if I die in this very moment, I will die a happy man. Not that dying is an option at this particular point in time. We have a marriage to consummate, and I have some pretty good ideas about how I plan on doing that.

As visions of our honeymoon start to dance across my mind, I feel that all too familiar movement in my pants. Alexis feels it, too.

'Your feet are not the only thing dancing right now, are they?'

I laugh and press her harder to my front. 'No, they are not.'

She stretches up, her face now level with my own, prompting me to lift her off the ground. I don't hesitate, gripping her tighter and raising her up, her feet now dangling centimetres from the floor. She kisses me hard and, during that kiss, it's as though we are the only two people in the room. We move across the floor to the music, her feet dangling, her arms wrapped around my neck, my lips and tongue still connected to hers — I'm the happiest I have ever been.

Hearing the song subside and Derek's voice no longer singing, we both open our eyes and come back to the moment.

'Mrs Clark?' I ask, completely transfixed by her radiant aura.

'Yes?' she answers with a giggle.

'Nothing, I just wanted to say your name.'

Alexis blushes. *I fucking love it when she does that.*

'Did you just blush, Mrs Clark?'

Her blush and smile disappear. 'No, I don't blush.'

'Oh, yes, you do.' I chuckle at her obvious denial.

'I do not,' she states tersely, in her stubborn tone.

'Do you want me to prove you wrong, right here, right now?'

She blushes. *I rest my case.*

Derek interrupts our moment and asks if anyone else would like to join us on the dance floor. He then hands over the microphone to the lead singer of a band that we often play gigs with, and then makes his way toward Carly.

Before I know it, we are joined by our family and friends, even Arthur and Geraldine. Arthur gives me a fatherly slap on the back and kisses Alexis on the cheek with congratulations.

Once again, swaying with Alexis still happily content in my arms, I feel a tap on my shoulder.

'Do you mind if I cut in?' Rick asks, indicating that he wishes to dance with Alexis.

I give him a nod. 'Sure, I need to find that sister of mine anyway.' I lift Alexis' chin with my finger and press a quick kiss to her lips before leaving her to dance with her ex-husband.

***

Moments later, I find Lucy sitting with Nic and Alexander, Al driving his toy cars on top of the table. I pick up a car and perform a high speed manoeuvre then crash it into the one Al is holding. He laughs and yells 'Boom'.

'Luce, come and dance with me,' I request, gesturing toward the dance floor.

'Where's your wife? Your wife!' she squeals. 'How does that feel?' She stands up and gives me a quick hug.

I lean in closer. 'Fucking perfect. And she's over there, dancing with Rick.'

Lucy looks over my shoulder. 'Oh. Well, come on then, let's go and keep an eye on them.'

'I don't need to keep an eye on my wife,' I reassure her, knowing deep down that I will *always* keep an eye on my wife.

'Fine, don't. I'll keep my eye on her.'

And I know damn well that she will.

Shaking my head at my devoted sister as we start to sway to 'With or Without You' by U2, I tell her that she can finally stop looking out for me. 'You can stop with the creepy research now.'

'Never,' she cackles like an evil witch.

Knowing this request is falling on deaf ears, I change the tone of the conversation and squeeze her tight. 'Thank you.'

'For what?' she asks with incredulity as she tilts her head up.

'For always being there for me.'

'Bryce, it's the other way around,' she scoffs.

I pull her back to my body and spin us both around. 'That's what you think.'

'Okay, you don't have to convince me twice,' she answers nonchalantly but in a teasing tone. *Cheeky shit.*

I smile into Lucy's hair and, just as we are about to settle in, the music changes and I hear Alexis groan.

'You did this on purpose, Rick!' she exclaims with frustration.

I'm just about to head over there and see what fuck is going on when Rick laughs.

'I don't know what you're talking about,' he fires back, feigning surprise. Then, with a grin on his face he pulls Alexis to him and they both begin to jive to 'Jailhouse Rock'.

My tension alleviates.

'It's like riding a bike,' Rick teases.

'Have you ever tried ridin' a freakin' bike with a wedding dress and heels on?'

I laugh.

'She's got an answer for everything, hasn't she?' Lucy mutters with a smile while shaking her head.

'She sure has.'

'I'm so happy for the two of you. Mum and Dad would've loved her.'

'Yeah, I know.'

'Especially Mum.'

I pull Lucy in for another tight hug, when I notice Brayden spot the wedding cake. 'Shit! Got to go.'

I take off and catch him just before Jake does.

'Jesus, he's quick,' Jake complains, slightly breathy.

'Of course he is. He's going to play football for the Cats, aren't you, Bray?' I declare proudly, picking him up and placing him on my hip.

Brayden looks from the cake then to me and makes a 'meow' noise.

I laugh.

Screwing up his face, Jake smiles like the cheeky fuck that he is. 'Not if Lex has anything to do with it. According to her, he was born a Bomber like his siblings.'

'She won't have anything to do with it. Brayden *will* support the Cats.'

Jake belly laughs, 'Bryce, you are fucked,' he says, right before slapping me on the back and walking off. *Fucking smartarse!*

I like my brother-in law, but he is a cocky son of a bitch at the best of times.

***

It doesn't seem too long before Alexis and I are cutting our cake. My lips are deliberately pressed to hers, so that she cannot see what I have coming. 'Remember when you told me how much you loved cake and cream?' I whisper, still keeping her attention fixated on me.

'Yeah,' she blushes.

'Is this just as good?'

I quickly move my hand to her face and mush a bit of cake into her mouth, cream smearing on her nose and chin.

The room fills with laughter and shocked gasps, together with Tash's unmistakable bellow. ''Bout time someone gagged you, Lex.'

Alexis stumbles back in surprise, her eyes wide open, her mouth filled with cake and cream. 'You didn't just do that,' she mumbles as she closes her eyes and swallows her mouthful.

Laughing and somewhat surprised that I actually went through with it, I reply. 'Yeah ... I did.'

Her eyes flick open again, a renewed sense of retribution covering her face. *Crap! I'm going to fucking regret this.* She raises an eyebrow and forcefully ploughs her hand into the top of the cake, grabbing a fistful before taking a step closer to me. I know what she is going to do — obviously, I deserve it — and she looks so damn sexy, I'm willing to let her.

Standing my ground and waiting for the cake to make contact with my face, I refuse to remove my stare from hers. She stops directly in front of me, now only mere centimetres away, her eyes searing me with lust. Then, like the tempting seductress that she is, she lifts her hand and licks the cake off her fingers ... slowly.

'Mm,' she moans quietly. 'This cake and cream is the *best* I've ever had.'

I watch her sensually devour her cream-covered digits with her tongue. *Fuck! Why are we in a room full of fucking people right now?*

'Mrs Clark,' I warn, my voice now gravelly from the lack of moisture that Alexis so easily strips me of.

'Yes?' she mumbles, swallowing her cake and smiling at me victoriously.

'I fucking love you,' I whisper aggressively, grabbing her neck and pressing her cake-smeared mouth to mine, the taste of her mixed with vanilla sponge and cream.

The room breaks into applause, Tash's wolf-whistle dominating the sounds that follow. Nate also voices his opinion that our cake-mushed kiss is 'gross'.

I couldn't care less though, wanting nothing more than to taste my wife, and considering I am not currently in a position to taste other parts of her body, I am more than happy to continue tasting her mouth.

***

As the evening progresses, Alexis switches between mingling with our guests and occupying the dance floor. I, on the other hand, switch between the mingling and watching her.

Alexis, Nate, Charli, and Brayden are all dancing in a circle, encouraging Brayden to bring his moves, moves he got from me. I especially like to take responsibility for the little hip and slide action he is currently performing. I let out a laugh and take a swig of my beer.

'Little tacker dances like his uncle,' Jake says proudly, snapping me out of my loving gaze.

I raise my eyebrow at him. 'You dance?'

'I put Patrick Swayze to shame.'

Coughing then choking on my beer, I call his bluff. 'Bullshit! You look like you have two left feet.'

'Don't bait me, Clark. I wouldn't want to show you up on your big day.'

This time I laugh loudly. 'Not going to happen, Jakey Snakey,' I taunt him, Jakey Snakey being Alexis' pet name for her brother, the same pet name Brayden now uses for his uncle. And a pet name I know Jake hates.

He slams his beer down on the nearest table. 'I fucking warned you.' He smiles, then takes off toward the band. I watch with curiosity as he says something to Simon, the lead singer.

Seconds later, the unmistakable sound of the drums in 'Need You Tonight' by INXS sound throughout the room. Alexis and Jen's heads both prick up like meerkats, then they spot Jake walk toward the centre of the dance floor. The smile that spreads across my wife's face indicates she knows what is about to happen.

Jen wolf-whistles and shouts, 'Lexi, get over here.'

Squealing, Alexis meets my eyes and gives Brayden a gentle push on the bum, steering him toward me. And, without further encouragement, he launches himself in my direction at full speed. *I swear to god, one and a half year olds do not know how to walk. Run ... yes; walk ... no.*

I gather him up and throw him into the air before catching him again, the sound leaving his mouth as he soars above my head, the best fucking sound in the world — I could listen to my son giggle 24/7.

'What are Mummy, Aunty Jen and Uncle Snakey up to?' I ask as I walk closer to the dance floor which is now circled by our family and friends.

'Sssssss snake,' Brayden hisses.

I laugh. 'Yes, snakes go hiss.'

He screws his face up all serious-like. 'Woof, woof. Grrr.'

'Are you a cat?' I enquire.

Brayden bursts into laughter and playfully slaps me on the forehead. 'Sill-ee dadda. Bayden a dog.'

'Oh ... of course you are.' I fake stupidity as I kiss him on the cheek.

Lifting my head to look over everyone else's, I spot Alexis and Jen performing simultaneous dance moves as Jake dances his way around the inside of the circle. I have to admit, he isn't bad, sliding when the lyrics suggest, then moving quite raw when the lyrics suggest that.

Johanna — Jake's girlfriend of two years — snorts and giggles as he drags her out into the centre of the circle. Then, lifting his eyebrow up at me in a watch-this-you-motherfucker kind of way, he swings Johanna's arms around his neck and starts dirty dancing with her, Patrick Swayze-style. I shake my head then salute him. *Cocky prick!*

***

After the speeches are said, the bouquet tossed and caught by Carly, and Alexis' electric blue garter is removed by my teeth, I can quite happily admit that I've had enough. I now want nothing more than to have Alexis all to myself. I want to spend the next eighteen hours — the approximate time it takes to fly to Paris — buried deep inside her, underneath her, on top of her and wrapped around her.

I can't wait. She is going to flip when she finds out where we are going but, as per usual, she will not find out until we are there. Part of the fun is going to be teasing and taunting her and, if I'm lucky, she will put up a fight. A fight I look forward to winning.

Now eagerly wanting to wrap up our celebrations and jet off to France, I search the room for my bride, finding her sitting with her girlfriends. I head in her direction.

Tash and Jade's expressions as I approach the table have me a little confused. Tash has a shit-eating grin, and Jade appears to be contemplating whether or not to jump off a cliff. But it's Carly's not so subtle indication to Alexis, using a slash-of-the-throat gesture, that she should cease her words, has me concerned the most.

'I hope he doesn't want to divorce me when —' Alexis says, stopping mid-sentence as I come to a halt right behind her. 'Shit! He's right behind me, isn't he?' she stutters.

'Why would I divorce you?' I whisper into her ear as I wrap my arms around her. 'I've only just married you.'

She stiffens in my arms, making my unease heighten.

'I ... I ... I did something yesterday, and I'm not sure if you'll like it or not. You may file for divorce.'

CHAPTER EIGHTEEN

'What did you do?' I ask, not really caring what she did. There's no way in hell I'd want a divorce. I've waited three years to make her my wife.

'I can't tell you. It will have to wait until later.'

I spin her around to face me. 'I will never divorce you, so give me your worst.'

'It's really not that bad. Well, I don't think it is. You might, though. And if you do ... well ...' She starts to stutter nervously again, so I lean in and kiss her, cutting off her babbling words.

'Shh,' I whisper against her lips as I break our kiss. 'We can talk about it later, but for now I want to take my wife on a plane and have her scream her husband's name over and over.'

'Mm, anything you say, you incredibly sexy husband.'

Opening her eyes as if she has just awoken from a trance, she pulls away from me, her mouth wide, her expression embarrassed. I can't help but chuckle.

'Shit! I just said that out loud, didn't I?'

'Yes, you did,' I explain. 'Come on. Let's say our goodbyes.'

Pulling her to my side where she fits perfectly snug under my arm, she rests her head against my shoulder as we walk.

'I'm going to miss the kids. I hope Brayden will be okay staying with Mum and Dad.'

'He'll be fine,' I reassure her, squeezing a little tighter, when truth be told, I have the same uncertainties.

ATTAINMENT

We both take a seat at our table, and Alexis puts her arms out for Brayden, who is sitting on Graeme's lap. 'Give Mummy a big cuddle, BB,' she mumbles into his neck as they bear hug each other.

I automatically clench both my fists, that being my natural reaction to the annoying nickname. But, unfortunately, due to underestimating her ability to pull one over on me, as it stands at this point in time that bloody nickname is not going anywhere.

'You be a good boy for Nanny and Poppa, and Mummy and Daddy will see you in a couple of weeks, okay?'

'He'll be fine, darling. Poppa has some "farmy stuff" we can do to keep us busy, don't we, Bray?' Graeme explains, using his code for farm slavery.

'I am not cleaning out the chicken coop again. That was disgusting!' Charli complains.

'I'll mow the lawns,' Nate pipes in, knowing that particular job comes with driving the ride-on mower.

Graeme laughs. 'See, they'll be fine. Go and enjoy yourselves.'

We hug all three kids and say goodbye before walking through a guard of honour.

***

'Are you going to tell me where are we going yet?' Alexis asks, unlatching her seatbelt as Paul — the plane's captain — has just informed us we can do so.

Following suit, I remove my belt and stand up. 'No. You'll find out when we get there.'

'Fine, I won't tell you my surprise then,' she pouts with a smile.

I offer her my hand and pull her up to stand flush with my chest.

'Thank you,' she says, like a stubborn child, and then turns her back to me. I follow closely behind as she walks toward the bedroom, and even though she is clearly shitty due to my refusal to disclose our location, her leading me to our bed is evidence she still wants to make love. I smirk at her cuteness and then place my hand at the top of her arse, firmly guiding her.

She instantly pulls away and winces, sidestepping from me and displaying an expression of discomfort.

'What's wrong, honey?' I ask while reaching for her hand.

'Nothing,' she responds with a fake smile, now stepping backward toward the room.

'Alexis, why did you just flinch when I touched you?'

'Bryce, where are we going?' she answers my question with a question, frustration in her tone.

Her defiance sends a surge of adrenaline coursing through my body and, together with my increasing need to make love as husband and wife, has me stalking her predatorily while displaying a hungry expression.

Noticing my lascivious prowl, she backs herself into the room, inevitably jailing herself. 'Bryce,' she says with less conviction, 'tell me where we are going.'

I shake my head from side to side, slam the bedroom door behind me, then remove the space between us.

Now holding her body against the wall with my own, I pose my question again, deliberately breaking it down for her. 'Why,' I whisper into her ear, 'did,' I say, breathing into her neck, 'you,' I growl, as I lick the top of her cleavage, 'flinch?' I ask as I spin her around and splay her hands against the wall.

Her fingers claw into the panels as I press my erection against her arse. 'Where are we going?' she probes again, still persistently holding her own.

Her fight has me hard as a fucking rock. 'Fine, have it your way,' I advise, as I slowly unzip the back of her dress.

Alexis changed out of her wedding gown right before we left for the airport, her attire now a red mid-length strapless number.

I finish undoing the zipper and begin to peel the dress from her body when she stops me. 'Bryce, wait!' Sucking in a breath, she turns her head to the side and closes her eyes as she breathes out. 'I love you.'

By this point, I have a pretty good idea of what she has done and, to tell you the truth, I'm fucking excited to see exactly what she chose. 'Honey,' I say as I remove her dress completely, letting it fall to the ground, 'I love you, too.'

Taking a step backward, I spot the freshly inked area at the base of her back. It looks a little raw. I drop to my knees, now face level with her tattoo and take in the scripted name and picture.

'Brylexis,' I read aloud, as I trace the letters without touching the mark.

Under our name is a picture of a star.

'Do you like it?' she asks, clearly hesitant.

'Yes,' I hiss. *Do I fucking like it? I more than fucking like it. It's one of the sexiest things she has ever worn.*

She breathes out as her body relaxes. 'Oh, thank god!'

Gripping her arse cheeks with both my hands, I lean forward and trail my tongue around the area, prompting her to tense up again and suck in another breath.

'I love it,' I growl.

Alexis widens her stance just a little, and that slight opening of her legs — an invitation to deepen my exploration — sets a fire within me. I can't help myself and I grip her G-string, tearing it apart before nipping and biting at her soft rear.

'Oh, god, Bryce,' she moans.

'Turn around,' I demand, my tone not one to be argued with.

Slowly, she does as she is told, and even though I love her tenacity at times, her submission is also just as pleasing.

Now staring at her naked flesh before me, I wet my lips in preparation for her taste, fervently anticipating our union.

'Foot,' I request, keeping my eyes on her moist pussy.

She obliges and lifts her heeled foot, placing it on my knee. While I remove her shoe, I trail my tongue up and down her leg, tantalising every nerve ending I possibly can.

'Other one,' I demand, repeating the same action.

With her shoes discarded, I lean forward and lash her clit with my tongue then trail it up her abdomen and in between her breasts until I'm at her mouth. I bend down, slide my arm behind her thighs, and lift her into my arms.

'Where are we going, Mr Clark?'

'To the bed, Mrs Clark.'

Almost instantly, I feel my bottom lip between her teeth as she holds it, stretching it slightly and taking it with her as she pulls away from my face. Her eyes display a mischievous retribution as she lets go, the feeling mildly uncomfortable, yet erotic.

'That's not what I meant, and you know it,' she says with a slightly annoyed tone.

'I know nothing of which you speak.'

'I hate you.'

'You love me.'

'No, I don't. Not right now.'

Laying her down on the bed, I climb over the top of her and look deep into her crystal-clear blue eyes that reveal her innermost feelings. When I pay attention to them, they never lie.

'Not right now?' I question, leaning forward to tenderly kiss her lips.

Pulling away from her perfectly fucking kissable lips, I wait for her answer.

'No,' she answers, her response obviously artificial.

I swipe her peaked nipple with my tongue before sucking on it, deliciously. 'How about now?' I prompt.

'Uh-uh,' she answers on an intake of air.

'Hmm. No?' I mumble as I switch breasts, only to tweak with my fingertips the wet, hard nipple I just abandoned.

Trailing my tongue further down her stomach, I dip it into her bellybutton then comfortably position myself between her legs. I smile victoriously as I take in the sight before me, seeing just how turned-on she is — the proof is in the pussy.

Her entrance glistens with arousal, moistened, the view parching my mouth. I swallow heavily and drag my finger along her clit, making circles also. 'How 'bout now?'

Her back bows, affording me a stunning view of her chest, but she still refuses to give in.

Having had enough of this game, I go in for the kill, hungrily devouring between her legs. I lash at her clit with my tongue while sliding two fingers into her pussy, moving them in a 'come hither' motion.

'Oh, Bryce,' she moans, her sultry sound eliciting a reverberating groan from within me.

'Do you love me now?' I growl, still pressing my lips to her wet clit.

'Yes ... yes, I always love you, every second of the day,' she admits, her voice rising along with her impending climax.

Satisfied pleasure rushes through me hearing her say those words. They never get old; I never tire of hearing her say them. Now, feeling overly fucking thrilled with her surrender, I suck her clit into my mouth, knowing this will tip her over the edge. I then wait for her body to relax as she comes back down to earth.

Sitting up on my knees, my cock is hard and heavy with desire, desire I want nothing more than to release into my wife. 'Come here,' I say, taking her hand and lifting her to her knees.

She looks down at my erection and a pleased appreciation washes over her face. It's the best fucking expression imaginable. Nothing tops the look she gives me when she admires my cock.

Scooting forward on her knees, she takes me in her hand, squeezing my base and dragging her hand to the tip. Her milking action is rewarded when a bead forms on my crown. 'Taste it,' I suggest, knowing that she wants to.

She smiles and sticks out her tongue, then leans forward and slides it along my sensitive head. I jerk with pleasure. She pumps once more in hopes of another bead and is rewarded when yet again one appears.

'Fuck, honey. Come here.' I pull her close and lift her up, impaling her on my shaft, both of us moaning in succession. I seize her arse with my hands and lift her up and down, thrusting with passionate dedication over and over.

She cries out with exertion as she reaches another climax, the sheer carnality of her scream a fucking pleasure to watch. The way her head falls back under the weight of physical pleasure and mental emotion rewards me for my efforts. I release one hand from her hip and clasp the back of her head, bringing it back to mine. Then, delving my tongue deep into her mouth, I expel my own orgasm.

We both collapse on the bed, thoroughly sated and fucked, and that wonderfully gratifying feeling of attainment washes through me. After seconds of catching our breath, I tug her to my side where she comfortably rests her head on my chest.

Gently, I kiss her on the head. 'So, how does it feel to be Mrs Clark?'

'Perfect,' she replies then hugs me tight.

***

Hours later, we are departing the plane and stepping onto the tarmac at Charles de Gaulle Airport. It's fucking freezing, the icy chill in the air piercing my skin like a thousand tiny needles.

'Paris?' she asks, spinning to face me and seeming unfazed by the near zero degree temperature.

The sheer excitement that is radiating from her fills me with so much joy. 'The one and only,' I reply, intertwining my fingers with hers, wanting to keep us both warm.

'Oh my god! Can we go see the Eiffel Tower, now?'

Personally, I want nothing more than to cuddle up to her naked body, the flames of an open fire dancing before our eyes. Except, seeing her exhilaration — that resembles a kid at Disneyland — I'm now more inclined to freeze my arse off just to continue witnessing her expression.

'If you want, but it's bloody cold,' I shiver, cursing myself for not having our coats accessible.

'Screw the cold. Paris blanketed in snow is so romantic. It is the only place in the world I would be happy to freeze to death.'

Shaking my head, I lead her toward the waiting limousine, hellbent on not allowing any freezing of her body to occur. 'We can go, see and do whatever you want. Our honeymoon is your oyster.'

She stops once again and I refrain from rolling my eyes, when I see her smile widen beyond normal proportions.

'Anywhere?'

'Yes, honey, anywhere but here. Come on, let's go see *La Tour Eiffel*,' I entice, my French rolling from my tongue.

'*Oui, s'il vous plaît, Monsieur* Clark,' she responds, her French spoken just as perfectly.

I groan at the sound of her words which are like verbal sex to my ears. 'Limousine. Now!'

***

Reaching Champ de Mars without burying myself inside Alexis was an impossibility. Her French words as I bucked my hips and she rode me were fucking sensational. '*Oh dieu, oh dieu,*' she'd chanted at my request. Followed by '*Oui, oui*', and finishing off with '*baiser*'. Needless to say, it was the best forty-five minute drive I have ever experienced.

Standing at the base of the monumental structure that is the Eiffel Tower, I watch with joy as Alexis arches her head back to get maximum perspective. Her obvious excitement feeds my delight, and I can't help but take a moment to absorb what my life now encompasses. The exquisite creature before me, my wife, is the woman who breathed life back in to me, giving me purpose to my existence and the desire to enjoy the life I have. She tempts me, satisfies me, fulfils me in every possible way. She is my greatest achievement.

Reaching into my coat pocket, I pull out a rose I had our chauffeur obtain for me, then take a hold of Alexis' hand, tugging her to my chest. Her eyes sparkle when I place the flower on her forehead and drag it down the bridge of her nose, her sight never leaving mine, not even for a second. Once I have trailed the rose across her lips, I lean forward and replace it with my mouth, sealing us with a passionate kiss. She is mine, and she always will be.

I have attained my ultimate perfection.

EPILOGUE

'Mum! Dad! Come on,' Brayden calls from the lounge room. 'Whatever it is you are both doing up there, stop. We're waiting for you.'

Nate, Charlotte, and Brayden all roll their eyes with a knowing smile, their mother and father's frequent disappearances a common occurrence in their household.

'Listen to this riff I've been practising,' Brayden says to his nineteen-year-old brother before diving right in to some guitar chords.

Nate looks up from tuning his axe, impressed with Brayden's ability to compose so simply, this natural talent obviously passed down from his father. 'Not bad, little bro.'

'I like it, Bray. Are you going to show Mum and Dad?' Charlotte asks before returning to warming up her vocal chords by humming her scales.

'Not yet, it's not finished.'

All three of them continue to prepare their instruments as Bryce and Alexis watch adoringly from the upper level. Bryce, having just listened to Brayden's roughly composed riff, couldn't be more proud of his eight year-old son. In fact, he couldn't be more proud of all his kids. He never saw Nate and Charlotte as his stepchildren, having always loved them as a father should.

'He's so much like you,' Alexis says to her husband of seven years while dropping her head to his shoulder. Every time she is faced with her youngest child, she is reminded that he is the epitome of his dad. This is both a good and bad thing where she is concerned.

'Yeah ... well ... he has to get his talent from someone,' Bryce playfully boasts, knowing Alexis will fight back. He adores it when his wife puts up a fight; he always has and he always will. Baiting her is one trick he has perfected over the years when wanting to be buried inside her, his taunts always resulting with them both passionately making love.

'Oh, so I am talentless, am I?' she says as she turns to face him. 'What I just did to your cock was something taught in everyday school, then?'

'Fuck! I should hope not,' Bryce laughs.

'I can guarantee, Mr Clark, that what my mouth is capable of is more than just a talent.'

Bryce pulls his wife to his chest and nudges her nose with his own. 'I know, my love. It's a gift.'

'Mum! Dad! Hurry up!' Brayden bellows.

'We're coming,' Bryce retorts.

Laughing, Alexis pulls away to join her children downstairs.

'Where are you going?' Bryce asks, securing his wife's back to his chest. 'I said we're coming and I didn't mean it in an adjectival sense.'

Alexis' body ignites, a natural reaction to her husband's dirty and promising words. 'We've come twice already. A third time is a bit greedy, don't you think?'

'I'm a voracious man.'

'I know, but your voracity will have to wait. We have three eager youngsters down there who want to jam with their parents.'

A battle of choices creates a dilemma within Bryce's mind, because he has to choose between his two favourite pastimes; making love to his wife, and jamming with his family. Knowing deep down that his commonsense will prevail over his lasciviousness, he lightly nibbles Alexis' ear and then lets her go. 'I know. Come on then.'

Bryce seats himself at the piano, now feeling comfortable playing after so long. He had refused to touch the keys following his mother's death, feeling the attempt to be too painful. But when he'd asked Alexis what she wanted for their one year wedding anniversary, she had said just one thing. 'Play the piano for me. It's time, my love.' Ever since that night, he has found a renewed love for the instrument and no longer feels the heart-wrenching pain he once did.

Pressing the keys to begin the song, he looks at Charlotte sitting beside him. On perfect cue, she begins to sing the lyrics to 'Fix You' by Coldplay.

When Alexis hears the first song that she sang to her husband many years ago, she nearly chokes on the emotion she holds so deeply for this man who she risked everything to be with. A man she was inevitably drawn to and could not be without, a man who is and always will be her soul mate. Standing behind him, she leans into his back and drapes her hands down his chest, resting her chin on his head as she joins in and sings with her daughter.

***

The moment Alexis presses herself against Bryce's back and her beautiful voice fills his ears, he knows he has picked the perfect song. His wife and stepdaughter sound like angels, the perfect accompaniment to the piano notes filtering the air. But it isn't until the chorus when both Nate and Brayden join in with their guitars, that Bryce truly appreciates his life. He honestly feels that he is the luckiest man alive, and for someone who never believed in luck, this sentiment in itself is a true testament to how far he has come.

His life, his wife, and his family, are his ultimate attainment.

ATTAINMENT

Turn over for a sneak peek at *Attraction*, the fifth book in The Temptation Series by KM Golland

ATTAINMENT

ATTRACTION (Book 4 in The Temptation Series)

PROLOGUE

Carly

Have you ever thought that you knew exactly where your life was headed? Knew what you would be doing and who you would be doing it with? Well, I did. I had my life somewhat mapped out in my head. My life was going to be free, free from obstructions, free from drama, and free from anchors that tied me down to anyone or anything. Yep, I was an anchorless ship on her maiden voyage that never ended.

I was going to sail through life on a continuous journey of good times, fashion and fun. I was carefree, fat-free, child-free and fancy-free. I had good health, good family and friends, good shoes, and a good arse! My life was good. Uncomplicated. That was until I met Derek.

Firefighter-Derek. Drop-dead-gorgeous Derek. Brown-eyed-dirty-talking-cocky-as-hell Derek. He was the sweetest man I'd ever met and the one person to completely change my infinite voyage of freedom.

He was my iceberg.

ACKNOWLEDGEMENTS

As always, I need to first and foremost thank my husband and children. Thank you for tolerating the long hours I put into my writing. For tolerating my crabby attitude when I have not allowed myself enough sleep. For tolerating the fact I have been so submerged in writing that I have forgotten to pick up fresh bread and milk. And, for tolerating the constant sight of me in PJs with a laptop permanently attached to the tips of my fingers.

To the three loves of my life ... I adore and appreciate your toleration of our new-found lifestyle. I adore and appreciate YOU. ♥

Mum and Dad, your support means the world to me. Thank you for always being just a phone call away, no matter what time of the day or night.

To my gorgeous and outrageous friends: Franny, Lea Lea, Gab and Renee. You provide the perfect balance of support when needed: a shoulder to cry on with frustration, an ear for listening when I'm confused and shitty, and a night out to make me laugh. But most importantly, your friendship and encouragement are a blessing.

Sarah, once again your comments and advice during the beta reading process are not only extremely helpful but incredibly hilarious. One of the thrills I get when writing 'The End' is not only the satisfaction of finally finishing my book, but the knowledge that your feedback is not too far away.

To my totally awesome and wonderful fans, thank you so much for all your beautiful messages and constant encouragement; for your fantastic reviews and for spreading the word. I have enjoyed creating and delivering Brylexis to you and adore the fact you love them as much as I do.

AUTHOR BIO

KM Golland was born and raised in Melbourne, Australia. After studying Legal Practice for two years and working as a Land Conveyancer for four years, she put her career on hold to raise two beautiful children. Always having a love for reading, she decided that rather than returning to the Legal Industry, she would become a Writer—self-publishing her debut novel Temptation (Book 1 in The Temptation Series.)

"I am an author. I am married. I am a mother of two adorable little people. I'm a Bookworm, Craftworm, Movieworm, and Sportsworm. I'm also a self-confessed Shop-aholic, Tea-aholic, Car-aholic, and Choc-aholic".

You can find K.M. Golland at:

http://www.kmgolland.com/

Goodreads:
http://www.goodreads.com/KMGolland

Facebook:
https://www.facebook.com/KMGolland?ref=tn_tnmn
https://www.facebook.com/temptationseries?ref=hl

Twitter:
https://twitter.com/KellyGolly

Made in the USA
Charleston, SC
22 June 2014